The MYSTERY of the

The MYSTERY of the

FROZEN BRAINS

Marty Chan

thistledown press

National Library of Canada Cataloguing in Publication

Chan, Marty
The mystery of the frozen brains / Marty Chan.
ISBN 13: 978-1-894345-71-2
ISBN 10: 1-894345-71-1

1. Chinese Canadians–Juvenile fiction. I. Title.
PS8555.H39244M98 2004   jC813'.54   C2004-900867-6

Cover illustration by Laura Lee Osborne
Cover and book design by J. Forrie
Printed and Bound in Canada

Thistledown Press Ltd.
633 Main Street
Saskatoon, Saskatchewan, S7H 0J8
www.thistledownpress.com

Canada Council   Conseil des Arts   SASKATCHEWAN   Canadian   Patrimoine
for the Arts   du Canada   ARTS BOARD   Heritage   canadien

We acknowledge the support of the Canada Council for the Arts, the Saskatchewan
Arts Board, and the Government of Canada through the Book Publishing Industry
Development Program for our publishing program.

ACKNOWLEDGEMENTS

My thanks to: Michelle for her unconditional love and support (I'll try to keep the toilet seat down); Jay Enright for being my first best friend; Wayne Arthurson for pointing the way; R.P. MacIntyre for guiding me to the finish line; Brad Smilanich and Danny Chan because you're my good luck guys; Kenda Gee for convincing me to write about my childhood; the gang at CBC Radio Edmonton for airing my childhood stories; Maureen Thomas, Nancy Musica, Wai Ling Lennon, the elementary students at Dovercourt, Kildare and Meyonohk (my test audience). Finally, Mom and Dad, thank you for being good sports.

ONE

I hated secrets. The thought of hiding the truth just made my stomach turn. Whenever I had a secret, I felt like a criminal. I felt like I was doing something wrong. Something horrible. The bigger the secret, the harder it was to hide, and I sat on an elephant of a secret. If anyone ever found out, the world would change forever. That's a very long time in my books.

I figured the best way to hide the secret from the world was to hide myself from the world. I became a shy, quiet nine-year-old wallflower. I never talked to anyone. I never made a peep in class. I never played with other students at recess. The price of protecting my secret was eating lunch alone. I paid the price without question, as long as my secret was safe.

Then my grade three teacher, Mrs. Connor, changed everything with one question. Little did she know that her question shook the castle walls that I had built around the truth. The dark, terrible truth about me, Marty Chan.

Mrs. Connor had asked the entire class, "What is the meaning of the word alienate?"

She adjusted her black glasses on the bridge of her hawk-like nose and scanned the classroom for someone to answer. If I looked at Mrs. Connor, she'd think that I wanted to answer. If I put my head down she'd assume that I didn't know, and she would ask me out of spite. I wished I could turn invisible, but I hadn't learned how to do that yet. Instead I stared in her general direction without making eye contact. I looked like I was trying to stare at the noon-day sun. I hoped my off-centre, squinty gaze would convince Mrs. Connor to pass me over. I did not want to answer her question.

I knew the meaning of the word, but I didn't want everyone else to know that I knew. "Alienate" was something you did to make everyone mad at you. I remembered the definition by breaking the word in half and adding an "h" to the second part — "aliens" were "hated."

If I answered right, I would alienate my classmates. They would give me strange looks, like they did when I first showed up at school. They would make up stories about the weird Marty. They would hound me and try to learn how I knew answers to Mrs. Connor's impossible questions. Eventually, they would discover my dark secret.

Mrs. Connor singled me out. "Marty, you know the answer, don't you?"

Everyone turned and looked. I turned into a bar magnet and my classmates became iron filings. I couldn't shake off their curious looks.

"Well," my teacher demanded.

Mrs. Connor was the toughest person in the entire school. She dished out detentions faster than you could blink. She sent kids to the principal for chewing gum in class. She yelled at people for even thinking about doing something bad.

One time she made Eric Johnson eat an entire bar of soap because he said something that sounded like a swear. Since then, no one ever stretched their mouth wide open with their index fingers and said "I was born on pirate ship." You did not want to make Mrs. Connor mad, so when she asked you a question, you had better say something to please her.

I looked into the narrow eyes of my teacher and stammered the answer: "Alienate is a verb that means to make someone unfriendly or hostile."

"Correct," she said.

The other kids were shocked that I had said something. They were even more shocked that I knew the answer. I felt my face burn from their probing stares.

Trina Brewster muttered "Smarty-Marty" and giggled.

The most popular girl in class, Trina was pretty, smart, and she wore cool clothes. Her dad owned the only swimming pool in Bouvier — my home town. Everyone wanted to be in Trina's good books, so when she started making fun of me, the others went along. They whispered Trina's new nickname for me and other unkind words.

Mrs. Connor growled, "Did I say you could talk?"

Dead silence. Everyone looked down. If Mrs. Connor wanted us to be quiet, she would ask a question. Normally people threw out questions to get other people to talk, but Mrs. Connor used questions to shut people up. She scanned the church mouse-quiet room with her owl eyes, poised to swoop on anyone who dared to squeak.

"You can spend the rest of the class reading chapter eight in your textbooks," she said.

She walked to the white board at the head of class. Behind her back, Trina screwed up her face and pretended to be Mrs. Connor. She wagged her finger at Eric Johnson and mouthed our teacher's last instruction to the class.

"That means silent reading, Miss Brewster," barked Mrs. Connor.

Our teacher had eyes in the back of her head, and she could hear better than a dog. She knew everything that happened in her class. If she knew that you had something to hide, she just kept picking on you until you gave up the secret.

Suddenly, Mrs. Connor looked at me and asked. "Why isn't your book open?"

Around me, everyone else had stuck their noses into their books. There were a hundred things I could have done. I could have opened my book and pretended to read. But Mrs. Connor had caught me off guard. I felt like she had just lobbed me a baseball. The right thing to do was to relax and catch it. But my hands had turned into pats of butter and I couldn't field the ball. All I could do was watch it fall on the ground.

"I'm done," I said.

Everyone gawked at me.

"Then read the next chapter," Mrs. Connor said.

"I'm done that one too," I said. Why couldn't I just shut up?

"Then keep reading, Marty."

"I'm done the whole book."

"Everything?"

I nodded. Around me, the kids muttered. I wished I could turn back time, but I hadn't learned how to do that yet. Whispered questions flew around the room. Everyone wondered how I could read so fast. Rumours would be close behind. The teasing would begin all over again.

Frustrated by her noisy students, Mrs. Connor decided to get rid of the cause. She turned to me and ordered, "Go to the storage room and do some free reading."

"But I'm done," I said.

"Read anything you want. Anything you haven't read yet. Go. Now!"

I yanked my Hardy Boys detective novel from the inside of my desk and got up.

Trina whispered, "He's not normal. He's a freak-a-zoid."

Everyone muttered in agreement. I bolted out of the room as fast as I could. My secret was no longer safe. I stomped into the hall, swung the classroom door shut. Then I stormed toward the storage room and shoved the door open.

"Ouch! Watch it," yelped a boy on the other side of the door. He straightened his red and blue Montreal Canadiens hockey jersey as he glared at me.

"I'm sorry," I said. "I didn't think anyone was in here."

"You dumb monkey butt," he said.

"Does it hurt?" I asked.

"Duh!" He rubbed his arm where the door had hit him and flinched.

"If it hurts when you touch it, don't touch it," I advised.

He pulled his straight brown hair out of his eyes and sneered, "It wouldn't hurt if you didn't push the door into me. Stupid Anglais."

I had heard that word before. The French kids called the English kids that, and they never said it with a smile. Anglais was not a compliment.

The French-Canadian students went to classes on the north side of my school, while my English-Canadian classmates studied on the south side. No one knew what happened on either side of the school. Rather than find out, people just made stuff up.

The English thought the French had magic powers that could turn people into frogs. The French believed the Anglais were cannibals that hungered for French meat. The only thing people knew for sure was that the French hated the Anglais, and the Anglais hated the French.

Every noon hour and recess, the Anglais and the French turned the schoolyard into a war zone. In the fall they pelted each other with crab apples. In the spring they soaked each other by kicking puddle-water. Now, in the middle of winter, they stockpiled snowballs for battle.

I didn't belong to either side of the war. I looked different from everyone else. I had black hair, dark skin, and my eyes were narrow like almonds. As much as they disliked each other, the kids hated me more. They called me names that made my eyes burn with tears and my neck feel all tingly and hot. I didn't want to go to school with any of them, but because I couldn't speak French, my parents sent me to school with the Anglais.

This meant that the boy in the Montreal Canadiens jersey was an enemy. His arms looked like they were cut from stone. Mine looked like they had been fished out of a pot of cooked spaghetti. One of his thighs was as thick as my entire body. He swung the storage room door closed and cracked his gigantic knuckles. I backed away.

The tiny room offered no hiding place. Shelves filled with school supplies surrounded us. The window had chicken wire across it. My enemy stood in front of the only escape route. I ran behind the giant wooden table in the middle of the room, keeping him on the other side.

"Maybe we can work this out. We don't have to fight," I squeaked.

"Are you stupid?"

I smiled. Unlike my cruel classmates, this guy thought I was dumb.

"I'm gonna wipe that goofy grin off your face," he threatened.

He snatched a white board eraser from the shelf behind him and hurled it. I ducked. It bounced off the wall. He grabbed textbooks and lobbed them across the table. None of them hit me. For the first time I was glad to be scrawny. I picked up a book to return fire. But as I cocked my arm back, Mrs. Connor stormed into the storage room.

"I could hear you from across the hall," she yelled. What are you doing in here?"

"We weren't doing anything," my French foe mumbled, acting like a captured soldier.

"Would you like to explain this to the principal?"

For an instant, the French boy and I were brothers-in-arms, pitted against a common enemy. Mrs. Connor had us in her sights, and her finger twitched on the trigger.

Suddenly words fired out of my mouth. "It was my fault. I was fooling around. Don't blame him."

The French boy shrugged, signalling that he agreed with my confession.

"I'm very disappointed in you, Marty," Mrs. Connor clucked.

"I'm sorry," I said. "It won't happen again."

"Get back to class."

"Yes, Mrs. Connor," I mumbled as I headed out of the storage room.

I looked back at the French boy, but he just glared at me. I was alienating everyone I met. I wished I could make friends, but I had not learned how to do that yet.

Two

By lunch time, Trina Brewster had spread rumours about me all over school. She took students on a freak-a-zoid tour, and I was the only attraction. Everyone crowded around my table in the middle of the cafeteria, while Trina fielded their many questions.

Eric Johnson shoved his way to the front of the group and asked, "Why is he so smart?"

Trina smirked, "Good question Eric. It's because he is a robot."

All the kids leaned forward and oohed. Eric Johnson rapped my head twice.

"Ouch," I said.

"Hey, he doesn't feel like a robot," Eric accused.

Trina quickly recovered, "That's because his brain is in his bum."

I got up, put my cafeteria tray behind me and shuffled out of the crowded room. Trina and her tour group followed me, searching for wires in my butt. Eric Johnson yelled out that he saw something. He stepped on a piece of toilet paper that was stuck to my shoe. The tour group jostled each other to get a closer look.

I scrambled out of the cafeteria and sprinted down the hall. I turned the corner and planted my face in the smelly T-shirt worn by Jacques Boissonault. I staggered back and saw the tall French boy brushing Marty germs off his shirt. Beside him, his twin brother Jean chuckled. The Boissonault brothers were the toughest guys in the entire school. They lived on a farm, and people said they were strong enough to tip their dad's cows off their hooves, and mean enough to do the same to humans.

"Stupid Chinaman," Jacques barked. "Watch where you're going."

Jean snickered. "He probably couldn't see where he was going because his eyes are always closed."

Jacques laughed. "They're not closed. They're just squinty."

"I'll be more careful next time," I mumbled. I walked away and let them talk to my back. Their bad words didn't sting as much when I walked away from them.

Jacques barked, "We're not done with you, Chinaman. Come back here."

Jean stopped his brother.

"Jacques, chill. The Rake's coming."

"Next time," Jacques yelled.

I turned to see the Boissonaults smile at Principal Henday, who everyone secretly called "The Rake."

"Good afternoon, Mr. Henday," the Boissonaults chimed in unison.

"Keeping out of trouble, boys?" asked the tall, reedy man.

"Yes sir," they said.

"Day's still young," he replied. "I'll be watching you both."

"Yes sir," the brothers mumbled, less polite.

Mr. Henday strolled into the cafeteria in time to slow Trina's tour. I scurried down the hall, careful to avoid bumping into anyone else. I kept one eye open for my new French enemy but saw no sign of him.

I hid in my homeroom class and read my Hardy Boys detective novel. Unfortunately, Trina found me and gathered her tour group at the doorway of the classroom. They jockeyed for the best sight line. Trina instructed everyone to closely observe my behaviour, as if I were some kind of caged bear. As Trina gleefully made fun of me, I wondered if I should have told Mrs. Connor about her trying to cheat off me last week.

The tour group timed how long it took for me to flip the page. They counted out the seconds so loud that I couldn't concentrate. Finally I just closed the book and put my head on my desk.

Trina said, "Now he's absorbing the book through his hair. They're like wires. That's why they're so straight."

The group wanted to know how I could be so smart. Trina claimed microchips in my forehead stored everything and pushed my eyes into their slanty shape. I wished I could shut my ears as easily as I could shut my eyes.

At the end of the day, I sprinted out of school like a wet cat scrambles out of a bath. I knew Trina's freak-a-zoid tour would probably follow me home, and I wanted no part of it. I knew my classmates would not stop until they discovered my secret. And worse of all, I knew my French foe would be looking for me.

My class let out a few minutes before the French classes. I stuffed my books into a paper bag and sprinted down the hall in my stocking feet. I slid to a stop in the boot room and jumped into my boots. Down the hall, Trina rounded up people for the freak-a-zoid tour. I hustled out of the building, but my boots were only half on. I scrunched my toes to hang on to the boots. Snow slid inside the boots and melted into my socks, which made everything icky and slowed me down.

I put my paper bag down and pulled my boots up. Behind me, Trina led her tour out of the building. However, Eric got bored of the tour and started to tickle Trina through her winter coat. She howled for help, and I wanted to rescue her. Her girl friends jumped into the fray and a tickle war started.

Before anyone spotted me, I snuck away with my bag of books. My parents refused to buy me a backpack because they wanted to save money. Instead, they made me use paper bags from their grocery store.

The bell rang to dismiss the French kids. I picked up the pace and used my chin to keep the top books from spilling out of my book bag, but I should have been more worried about the bottom. The bag burst open and the books rained to the ground.

I dropped to my knees. The cold bit into my legs. I ignored the pain and scooped up my books. I looked back for my French enemy. No sign of him. I piled my snow-covered books on top of each other and staggered to my feet. I trudged through the snow barely able to hold on to my books.

"Hey," a voice called out. "You! Wait a minute."

I looked back and saw my French foe marching after me. I kicked into high gear. I clutched my books tight to my chest as I ran to the gate in the chain link fence that marked the end of the schoolyard. I felt like Ichabod Crane, the character in my favourite cartoon. If I could just get to the fence, I would be safe. Then I remembered that Ichabod never got away. I decided to take the Legend of Sleepy Hollow off my list of favourites.

I reached the fence and leaned against the frosty links to catch my breath. I could barely hang on to my slippery books. My French enemy walked closer. He took his sweet time, because he knew he had me where he wanted me.

I pushed off the fence to run down the street, but my winter jacket was stuck. I leaned forward. The zipper of my jacket dug into my neck and pushed my Adam's apple up my throat. I snapped back and tried to shake myself loose. My books fell to the snow. I let out a wild howl and tried to yank myself free. I didn't budge. I was doomed.

"Didn't you hear me calling you?" my French enemy said.

I shook my head.

"Stupid," he growled. He flicked his hand toward my head. I closed my eyes and waited for him to strike. Time crawled by. Why was he taking so long?

Then I felt him grab my jacket. I flinched. This was it, or was it? I peeked out of one eye. My French foe stood in front of me, but his arms hung down by his side. His unclenched hands suggested he meant me no harm.

"Your jacket was stuck on the fence," he said. "Happens to me all the time."

I took a step forward and came free of the fence.

"Why did you do that?" I asked.

"In the storeroom, you didn't have to take the blame for me," he said. "I can take care of myself."

"Sorry. I won't help you next time."

"You aren't really on the Anglais side, are you?"

"Why?" I said.

"No Anglais would ever do what you did."

"So you're not going to beat me up?" I asked.

"I could if you want me to."

"No. No. It's okay."

My Hardy Boys detective novel began to slide off my pile of books. I caught it between my knees. I waddled through the gate. To the French boy, I must have looked like I really needed to pee.

"You need help?" he asked.

"I'm fine. I'm good. It's alright." Then the book fell to the ground along with the stuff in my arms. "Nuts!"

He bent down and helped me pick up the books. I looked back at the schoolyard. The French guys watched the tickle war, and paid no attention to us.

I nodded toward the schoolyard. "Aren't you afraid of what your friends will think?"

He shrugged as if he didn't care, but he stole a glance at his friends. No one looked our way. Then he said, "You aren't like the Anglais. You're something else."

I froze. Had he figured out my secret?

"You read all these books?" he asked.

"Yes."

"You're still stupid," he smiled. "You thought I was going to beat you up."

He was nothing like the Boissonault brothers. He wasn't like Trina or Eric, or all the kids who made fun of me.

"My name is Remi Boudreau," he said.

"Marty. Marty Chan."

"I heard about you. That little Anglais girl was getting people to follow you. She kept calling you a . . . a . . . what was it?

"Freak-a-zoid," I muttered.

"Yeah. That's it. Why did she call you that?"

"Because I can read fast and I know stuff."

"You mean because you're smart?"

"I guess."

"What a bunch of dumb monkey butts."

"You don't think I'm a freak?" I asked.

"Well, it would be nice to have someone help me with my homework."

"I can do that."

"So how come you're so smart?" Remi asked.

"I can't tell anyone."

"Come on. I bet your parents make you study all the time."

"Yes, but it's not that."

"You can tell me, can't you?"

"It's a secret," I whispered.

Remi's eyes lit up. "What kind of secret?"

When you tell someone you have a secret, they want to know all about it. The more you tell them that they can't know what you know, the more they want to know.

I remember last Christmas at my house. My mom had wrapped a present and stuck it under the kitchen table. We didn't have a Christmas tree, because Dad couldn't see the sense of having a tree around for just one month. Anyway, Mom told me not to open my present until Christmas. As soon as she said that, I had to know what was inside the colourful box. For three days I tried to sneak a peek at the present. I snuck under the table and pulled the wrapping paper off the box bit by bit, until the present looked like a mouse had been gnawing at it.

But I finally made enough of an opening in the wrapping paper to sneak a look inside the box. I was so disappointed. I went through all this work only to find a wool sweater.

I wondered if Remi would feel the same way about my secret. Maybe he would shrug off the truth with a "so what?" Maybe I had it all wrong. I wondered if I would have the same problems now if I had told everyone. But my secret was way bigger than a wool sweater.

"You can trust me," Remi said. "I promise I won't tell anyone."

"How do I know that?"

"I always keep my promises."

"You could be lying to me."

"Hey, I guess you're not that dumb after all."

"Forget it," I said. I started to walk up the street.

"Wait," Remi called after me. "How about I tell you a secret? If you find out I blabbed your secret, you can tell everyone about mine. Then we'd be even."

His offer sounded pretty good.

I said, "But it has to be a big secret. One that you don't want anyone to know about."

"Why else would it be a secret?" Remi said.

"I mean you would die if anyone else found out. That kind of secret."

"Okay, okay. You can't tell anyone else this. But I like the Toronto Maple Leafs."

"That's it?"

"What do you mean that's it?" Remi was shocked that I didn't think much of his secret. "If people at school found out, they'd kill me."

"Why?"

"I'm French. We cheer for one hockey team, and that's the Montreal Canadiens. They are supposed to be the only real hockey team. But I think the Maple Leafs are better."

"Then why do you wear the Montreal Canadiens jersey?"

"Duh! So no one will suspect, monkey butt," he said. "If you tell anyone, I'll body check you into tomorrow."

Remi's glare reminded me of the time I broke Dad's glasses, and he warned me to never play soccer inside ever again.

"I promise I won't tell," I said.

"You'd better not."

"Do you swear you'll keep my secret too?"

"I swear."

"Okay. There's a reason I look different from everyone else at school," I said.

"Yeah, you're Chinese."

"It's more than that."

"What?"

I took a deep breath and let out my big secret. "I am an alien."

THREE

Remi didn't believe me at first. He screwed up his face and tilted his head. He looked up and down me for some hint of alien.

"I know Santa Claus is real," he said. "Because I saw him in the mall. I've never seen an alien, and I don't think I see one now."

"What about God? Do you believe in Him?"

"Duh. Everybody does."

"But you can't see Him," I said.

"I see Him every day."

"How?"

"He's in my mom and dad. He's in you. And He's in the sky. He's in everything. That's what Father Sasseville says, and he's never wrong."

"Who's Father Sasseville?"

"The priest. Don't you go to church?"

I shook my head.

"What kind of person doesn't go to church?"

"An alien."

"Nice try," Remi said. "But can you prove it?"

"Come with me and I will, but we have to be careful. It might be dangerous."

"What kind of danger?"

"The dangerous kind."

Remi nodded. He seemed to like the idea of danger. "Okay, let's see this evidence."

"It's in my parents' store," I said.

"Sounds dangerous," Remi smiled.

The store sat in the centre of the town. At one time, everyone shopped at my parents' store, but since the IGA opened two blocks over, the centre of town shifted to the IGA, along with all my parents' customers.

"Wow, the building totally looks like a flying saucer," Remi joked.

I led Remi to a car parked across the street from my parents' shop. Behind us stood the hardware store where cool dads bought lumber, nails, and paint to build tree houses or go-carts for their kids. My dad just got sawdust from there. He claimed it helped keep the floor clean, but covering the floor with curly wood-shavings seemed weird to me. Alien-from-outer-space kind of weird.

"We have to figure out a way to get you inside," I said.

"Here's a crazy idea. How about I just walk through the door?" Remi smirked.

"That'll never work, Remi. My parents are suspicious of any kid who goes into the store. They'll watch you as soon as you get in there."

"I'll say I'm your friend."

"That's a terrible idea," I said. "It'll make them watch you even more."

"Your parents are crazy, and I'm not so sure about you."

"If you were secret aliens, wouldn't you be worried about people snooping around?"

Remi thought for a second, then nodded. "So how do I get past them?"

"Follow me."

I snuck along the street away from the hardware store to the bakery which had the best cream puffs in the entire universe. Remi and I stayed low, peeking from behind parked cars in case my parents were looking out the store window. We took turns making sure the coast was clear. Mr. Halston, the baker, spotted us from his shop window. He wiped his hands on his white apron and gave us a strange look. I nudged Remi and straightened up. He followed my lead. We sauntered to the corner, acting normal. We looked both ways then crossed the street.

"Where are we going?" Remi asked. "To Uranus?"

"Har, har."

"I love that planet," he chuckled.

We passed the medical clinic and the bank. Instead of taking the direct route to my parents' store, I led Remi the long way to the alley behind the store. The hard-packed snow squeaked under our boots as we walked through the snow to the double wooden doors at the back of my parents' store.

"Wait here. I'll open the doors from the inside," I whispered.

"Why do we have to be so secret?" Remi asked.

"My parents don't know that I know I'm an alien."

"How's that possible? Didn't you always know you were an alien?"

"No, I just found out a few weeks ago."

"Hold on. How can you not know that you're an alien? You are an alien or you're not." Remi crossed his arms and stepped back.

I said, "I don't have pointy ears or strange powers, if that's what you're wondering. But I do look different. I look Chinese.

"Duh. That's because you are Chinese."

"I used to think that too. I used to think that I was just going through a phase. When I got old enough, my hair would turn blond and I'd get blue eyes, and I'd look like everyone else."

"You're a monkey butt."

"What?"

"If you think I'm going to believe — "

"It's true," I interrupted. My skin is a disguise to cover up what I really look like. Just like my parents have a disguise."

"A disguise?" Remi was curious again.

"I never felt right being Chinese. Well, now I have proof that I'm supposed to look like something else. Except my parents covered my true face."

"Why would they do that?"

"I don't know. That's why I need your help. To find out the reason for all this."

"Why wouldn't your parents say you were an alien?"

"Maybe they're waiting for the right time so I won't be shocked."

"Marty, this reeks of monkey butt. It sounds really dumb."

"It'll make sense when you see my proof. Do you want to help or not, Remi?"

"It's still going to be dangerous, right?"

I nodded.

"Okay. But if you're wasting my time, you're gonna be sorry."

"You'll be amazed," I promised. "I'll be right back."

He hugged himself. "Hurry up. It's getting cold out here."

I sprinted to the front of the building. As I got closer to the glass doors, I slowed down and caught my breath. I had to pretend that nothing was wrong. If my parents suspected anything, I would not be able to sneak Remi inside. I could get past my dad no problem, but Mom was a different story. She knew exactly what I was doing at any time, especially when I was doing something I wasn't supposed to do. Her powers were different than Mrs. Connor's super hearing. Mom could read people's minds.

Last winter, I came down with a bad cold. I tried to hide it from Mom, but she detected my sniffles with her radar. She sat me down at the kitchen table, while she brewed a soup to cure my cold. Even with a stuffed up nose, I could smell the awful, thick, brown gunk. It tasted even worse. One sip nearly made me puke. Instead of swallowing, I sucked the awful liquid into my mouth until my cheeks puffed out. Then I pretended that I needed to pee. I ran from the kitchen into the bathroom, and spewed out the soup into the toilet. I kept loading up with soup and "peeing" it out, until the bowl was empty. But Mom knew what I had done. She told me to stop fooling around and poured more soup into the bowl. I had to gulp it down in front of her.

If I was going to sneak Remi into the store, I would have to block Mom's mind-reading powers. I filled my mind with all sorts of useless information. I counted the number of tiles in the floor. I thought about why the Boissonault brothers always liked looking at the women's underwear section of the Sears catalogue. I thought really hard about Trina getting a face wash so cold that it froze her jaw shut.

I headed past the counter where Dad read his newspaper as usual. These days, he had time to read all sorts of things, because the store was always quiet. I didn't think he had mom's mind-reading powers, or else he would have used them to figure out a way to attract customers.

"Hi, Dad. I'm home from school." I made small talk to play it cool.

Dad grunted. "Hurry up. You have work to do."

"Where's Mom?"

"She making dinner."

She worked in the home part of our store, out of mind-reading range. There, our family could hide from customers, if we had any. Although small, our home was comfortable. It had a kitchen, two bedrooms, and a bathroom, but no one ever saw this living area because it was hidden. By the same token, she couldn't see what happened in the store. She would not see me sneaking Remi inside. I started to jog to the back of the building.

"Where you going?" Dad asked.

I froze. Did he suspect? Normally, Dad cared more about the store and his customers than me. Today of all days, he decided to speak to me after weeks and months of barely saying a word. I forced an innocent look on to my face.

"I'm going to do my chores," I told my alien dad.

"With your jacket on?"

If I didn't think fast, my mission would fail, and Remi would freeze to death outside waiting for me.

"Uh . . . I was going to take out the garbage first." I hoped Dad wouldn't ask more questions, like why hadn't I taken out the garbage in the morning when I was supposed to.

"Don't take too long. And no playing in the snow."

I nodded. Then I rushed to the back of the store before he could ask any more questions. As I walked further away from Dad, I expected him to throw me another question. But he didn't. Getting Remi inside was going to be a breeze.

When I reached the back, however, my heart sunk. The door to our living area was wide open. I looked down the hall and saw my mom in the kitchen. She stood in the line of sight of the back doors. If I let Remi in now, Mom would spot him right away and chase him out. I had to close the kitchen door before I let Remi in.

I slunk toward the doorway, sliding along the cement wall. My winter jacket crinkled, sounding like thunder. I froze and closed my eyes hoping that if I didn't see Mom, she wouldn't see me. A moment passed. I popped one eye open and saw no one. I heard Mom chopping on the wooden cutting board. I smelled onions and pictured her cleaver dicing the green stalks. She chopped so fast it sounded like machine-gun fire.

All I had to do was pull out the wooden doorstop, and the door would swing shut by itself. This happened all the time, so Mom wouldn't think twice about it. As long as I could pull out the doorstop before she saw me, my plan would work. But I had to do it while I could still hear her chopping in the kitchen. No time to waste.

I pushed away from the wall and rushed to the door. I listened through the doorway. Mom had stopped chopping. I flattened myself against the wall. Footsteps clicked toward me. Mom was picking up my brain signals. I filled my mind with clutter: math problems, the intra-mural sports schedule, how I hated Trina but still wanted to smell her hair.

The footsteps stopped. I peeked around the corner and saw my parents' bedroom door swing shut. Mom had gone to get something from her room. It was now or never. I grabbed the wooden doorstop, but it was stuck. I pulled harder. It inched out, but still held tight. Then I saw the bedroom door creak open. Mom was on her way out. I yanked on the doorstop with all my might. The triangular block screeched against the wooden door, but finally came free. I scrambled back and hid against the wall. I heard Mom's footsteps in the hallway. Soon, the sounds of chopping began again. She hadn't noticed the door swing shut.

I tiptoed to the back doors. I carefully turned the deadbolt and opened one of the doors. Remi barged into the store and stamped his feet on the tiled floor, making a huge racket.

"What took you so — "

I clamped my hand over Remi's mouth. He struggled as I dragged him behind a stack of boxes and kicked the door shut.

I whispered, "My mom's down the hall. If she hears us, we're done."

Remi nodded. He pulled my hand away from his mouth. For a few minutes, all I heard was our breathing. I silently counted to ten. No sign of Mom.

I squirmed around Remi and stuck my head out from behind the boxes. The door to the kitchen was still closed. I quickly locked the back door. Then I motioned Remi to follow me down the hall.

"This is so cool," he whispered.

I gave him a thumbs up, then I zigzagged from one side of the aisle to the other, just like I had seen cops do on television shows. Remi copied me move for move. I guessed he must have seen the same shows. We snuck out of the backroom and crept into the main part of the store. I looked up and down the aisle. The coast was clear. I led Remi along the aisle toward the cookie section.

"What are we looking for?" Remi said.

"You'll see."

I knelt in front of a shelf full of dusty oatmeal-raisin cookies. No one ever bought these stale cookies, but my dad refused to take them off the shelf. He believed that they would sell one day. He came close to selling a package one time, when Jacques Boissonault needed a hockey puck for a pick-up game. I joked that he could use the super stale and hard oatmeal-raisin cookies. Dad jumped on the idea. Jacques growled that my dad would sell dust bunnies for a quick buck and stormed out of the store. No one wanted to buy these cookies, which meant that this shelf was a perfect hiding place.

I cleared the shelf and shoved my arm into the dark space. Remi looked at the cookie package and licked his lips.

"Mmm, good looking cookies."

"Are you nuts?" I said. "They're oatmeal-raisin."

"Really?"

"Yeah, the name's right on the package." I pointed at the giant letters across the cookies which looked deceptively tasty.

Remi shook his head. "I must have missed the title."

"How could you miss it?"

He avoided answering my question. "Ugh. Who eats oatmeal-raisin? It's like chewing mouse poo."

My hand fumbled along the wood grain of the shelf until it rested on something flat and smooth. I pulled out a glossy magazine.

"Put the cookies back," I told Remi. "Then I'll show you the proof."

Remi shoved the packages back on the shelf, then he followed me around the corner of the shelf unit so that no one would see us. Safely out of sight, I showed Remi the magazine — proof of my real origins. The cover showed a giant flying saucer hovering over a farm house. Remi looked at the picture and scratched his head.

"It's a U.F.O. magazine," Remi said. "That's all you got?"

"Yes," I said. "That's all I need."

"It looks kind of lame."

"Read page 17. There's an article about how to spot a real alien."

I had dog-eared the page so it didn't take Remi long to get to the article. On the page a drawing of a naked wrinkly alien with a big bald head and giant black eyes stared out at us. Underneath the sketch was the article I wanted Remi to read.

"See," I said. "I told you."

"So?"

"What do you mean so? The article will tell you everything you need to know about aliens."

Remi studied the picture. "It doesn't really look like you."

"Read it."

"This is dumb." Remi pushed the magazine away.

"What's the matter? This is my proof. Read it."

"It's too stupid."

"Just read it."

Remi threw the magazine on the floor. "Forget it!" He started to get up.

"Are you too dumb to read it?" I said.

"Shut up." He headed down the aisle.

I realized that I was the dumb one. Remi couldn't read the article because he didn't know how to read English. That's why he missed the label on the oatmeal-raisin cookies. He was too proud to tell me. I wished I could take back what I had said, but it was too late.

"Why don't I read it to you?" I offered.

He stopped and turned around. "You don't think I can read it myself? Is that what you think?"

"No, I don't want to waste your time. Come on, I'll just read you the important stuff."

Remi shrugged. "Whatever."

I picked the magazine off the floor. Remi sat down beside me and pretended to follow along in the article. I told him the high points. The magazine reported that aliens walked the Earth right under everyone's noses. They had disguised themselves. I stressed the word "disguised."

"Hold on. Wait a minute," he interrupted. "If you're in disguise, let's just pull it off."

"You don't think I've already tried?" I said. "I've spent hours in the bathtub trying to scrub off my skin."

"And did it work?"

"No. I think my parents used some kind of transformation ray. My disguise is something more than just a costume or a mask." I kept reading. "The magazine says if you know what to look for, you can see past an alien's disguise. There are three telltale signs. Number one, the eyes. Even if they wear a human disguise aliens can not hide their black, cat-like eyes. These dark orbs will instantly give away an alien. To compensate, most aliens wear glasses to make their eyes look wider."

I took off my glasses and showed Remi my narrow, black, cat-like eyes.

"It's just a coincidence," he said.

I kept reading the article. It stated that aliens built flying saucers that traveled across many galaxies in the blink of an eye. They constructed special tractor beams to lift cows up to their space ship. They made invisible clothes, which is why they always looked naked. The article said that only super-intelligent beings could build such incredible inventions.

I put the magazine down and said, "If they're super-smart, then they can read really fast. Just like me."

"It's another coincidence," Remi said, but he did not sound so sure of himself this time. "Keep reading."

The third telltale sign about an alien was their size. They were short and skinny so they could fit through their tiny spaceship doors, which had to be small to keep air from leaking out. The magazine stated that an alien looked like a small sickly child.

"Everyone thinks I look like a small sickly child," I confessed. "What other proof do you need?"

Remi shook his head. "I was hoping you'd show me a spaceship. That'd be real proof."

"I got something even better."

"What?"

"My mom," I said.

"How's that going to prove you're an alien? You said you're all in disguise."

"When you see how she behaves, you'll think differently."

"I don't think so."

"She might give us ice cream for dessert."

Remi's eyes lit up. "Well, maybe I can stick around and do some investigating of my own."

At the dinner table, my mom stared at Remi with the look she reserved for my dad when he came home late. She had reluctantly agreed to let Remi stay for dinner, after I told her that I was helping him with his homework. Mom never stood in the way of schoolwork, but she didn't trust Remi. She watched him closer than she watched potential shoplifters.

Remi didn't help matters. He took an instant dislike to my mom when she said only lazy people do poorly at school. He grumbled behind her back and grunted short answers to any questions Mom asked him. Finally, she gave up talking to him about her beliefs on school work.

"Set the table Marty," Mom ordered.

I went to the counter beside the portable stove and grabbed a handful of chopsticks from an empty peach can. I laid three pairs around the table and put one on the kitchen counter for Dad. He never ate with us because he had to mind the store. Mom always brought his dinner out to him.

Remi examined the wooden sticks. "What the heck do I do with these?"

"You eat with them," I said.

Remi held one chopstick in each hand and tried to figure out how to pick up food with them. At first, he thought they were spears, and he jabbed at imaginary bits of food. Then he thought he could use them like a warehouse forklift.

I picked up my chopsticks and showed him how to hold them properly in one hand, like two pens. He copied me, but his chopsticks jumped from his clumsy hand and spun to the floor.

"*Aiya, give your friend a fork,*" Mom said.

I nodded and headed to the kitchen drawer. Remi jumped up from his seat and joined me.

"What did she say?" he whispered.

"Didn't you hear her?"

"Yeah, but it was in Chinese."

"She said to get you a fork. Didn't you understand her?"

"Duh, I don't speak Chinese."

Something dawned on me. "How do you know it's Chinese and not an alien language?"

"I don't know. You're the one who's Chinese."

"Yeah, but isn't it weird that there are no other Chinese families in town?"

"I guess but what does it matter?"

"This way, my parents can speak alienese and people would just think it was Chinese."

Mom often used this language to talk about customers, so that my dad could understand her, but they could not. Most times she didn't have anything good to say about them.

"Maybe they're making notes on Earthlings," I said. "That's why they need to speak in alien code, and being Chinese is just a cover."

Remi took a long look at my mom.

I added, "And that's why there can't be other Chinese families in town. Because if there were, they'd learn that my family are really aliens."

Remi nodded his head slowly as the truth started to sink in. Any doubts disappeared when he saw what my mom served for dinner. She slapped two plates down on the dinner table. On one plate, chicken feet stewed in brown juices. The claws curled like little fists with sharp spurs. Octopus tentacles infested the other plate. They did backstrokes in a murky sauce.

"That can't be what I think it is," Remi said.

"What is wrong?" Mom asked.

"Where's the sweet and sour pork?" Remi asked. "Where are the dried spareribs? The pineapple chicken?"

I kicked Remi under the table, then smiled at Mom. "I told Remi we might get some of that here."

Mom glared at Remi, "This is all you get."

"But I can't eat all of this by myself," he squeaked.

"You don't have to," I said. I picked up my chopsticks and plucked a tentacle and deposited it on my bowl of rice. Then I plucked a chicken foot from the other plate and plopped it on top of the tentacle.

"Are you kidding?" Remi asked as if I had just grown a third eye.

I whispered, "Just eat before my mom gets suspicious."

Remi gulped and looked from the plate of chicken feet to the plate of octopus tentacles.

"Your friend not like my food?" Mom asked.

"He's not used to it," I said.

"Silly boy. Why did he want to eat with us then?"

"What did she say?" Remi asked.

"You don't want to know," I said.

Remi jabbed his fork into a chicken foot and held it up for inspection. He took one look at my mom and smiled. Then he tried to put the foot in his mouth. His hand shook and the foot fell on the dimpled card table. Remi scooped it up with his fork and tried again.

Mom hissed, *"Make sure he doesn't stay too long."* She put Dad's dinner on a tray and added her own dinner to it.

"Okay," I mumbled.

"I eat with your dad tonight," she said in English for Remi's benefit. Then she left.

Once Mom was gone, Remi dropped his fork and pushed away from the table. He looked white as a sheet.

He said, "I've been to Uncle Wong's Buffet Palace. I know what Chinese food is supposed to be, and it's not this."

"So now do you believe me?"

"This is so gross." Remi picked a tentacle off the big plate, but it slipped out of his grip and fell on the floor. He picked it up carefully.

"I saw this in my sister's science book. It's the arm of an octopus," he said. "And you eat it?"

"It's not that bad tasting," I said. "Try it."

`Remi brushed the dirt of the tentacle and then popped it into his mouth. Suddenly, his face scrunched up and he spit the tentacle out. It bounced on the table and landed in the claw of a chicken foot. Remi scraped his tongue with his fingers.

"Yuck," he gasped. "Give me some water so I can wash the taste out."

I grabbed a pitcher from the kitchen counter and poured a glass for Remi. He took one gulp and spit the water back into the glass. He put it on the table and pushed it as far away from him as possible.

"It's warm. Why is it warm?"

"It's boiled."

"I want cold water from the tap."

"We're not supposed to drink water from the tap," I said. "Mom says that tap water is unsafe. I can only drink boiled water."

Remi examined the glass of water, then eyed the food on the table. He shuddered. "Your family have to be aliens to eat this stuff. I believe you now."

FOUR

After dinner, Remi and I went to my room to look through the U.F.O. magazine. I propped a chair against the door in case Mom decided to check up on us. Remi couldn't get enough of the articles. He made me read them to him and he hung on every word.

"They cut up cows in the night?" he asked.

"Yes. But there's no blood or anything. Sometimes pieces of the cows are missing. And there's mysterious burn marks on the grass. Probably from the landing gear."

"Cool. What else do aliens do?"

I read Remi an article about how aliens were responsible for the Bermuda Triangle.

"I heard about that place. It's where all the boats and planes go missing. What do the aliens want with them?"

"It doesn't say."

"I'll bet there's a race of giant aliens, and they use the boats and planes as bath toys for a big alien baby. What do you think?"

"I think they...we...study them. Especially planes."

"Why?"

"Because no plane can ever catch a U.F.O. Maybe the aliens want to stay ahead of the humans."

"Yeah," Remi nodded. "That makes so much sense. They don't want to be caught."

"The magazine says that people only see the mysterious lights in the sky. No one has ever caught one of the flying saucers."

"Wow. What else?"

I read an article about how cars wouldn't start if a flying saucer hovered nearby. The magazine said that motors would mysteriously die.

"They sure like to use the word 'mysterious' a lot," Remi noted.

"Oh, check this one out," I said.

I showed Remi a drawing of two men in long black trench coats, their faces behind pulled-up collars. The men wore weird hats, which reminded me of the hats detectives wore in old black and white movies. The men wore sunglasses to hide their eyes.

"Who are these guys? They look mysterious."

I read the article aloud. "The greatest mystery about the aliens is the Night Watchmen. These seemingly normal human beings travel the globe to investigate U.F.O. sightings. Witnesses report that these Night Watchmen, always dressed in black, come out whenever a U.F.O. is spotted. They tell the witnesses to forget they saw anything, often intimidating the witnesses. Soon after the Night Watchmen leave, the U.F.O.s are never seen again in that area. However, witnesses do report the uncomfortable feeling of being watched."

"Wow," Remi said. "Does it say who the Night Watchmen are?"

"I think they're agents for the aliens. They make sure no one ever finds out that aliens are around. They protect the aliens."

"Are they from my planet or yours?"

"The article doesn't say."

"And they all look like this?"

"Yup."

"Cool. You ever see one?"

I shook my head. "I don't think I want to see one of them either. They sound pretty scary. The magazine says the Night Watchmen can be really mysterious."

Remi took the magazine and stared at the drawing of the Night Watchmen, trying to get a look at their hidden faces.

He turned to me. "There's one thing I still don't get. How come you didn't know you were an alien before you found the magazine?"

"I think I was born here."

"Then why didn't your parents tell you that you're from another planet?"

"I don't know," I said. "That's what I'm hoping to find out."

"Maybe they thought you couldn't keep a secret."

Remi's comment reminded me of the time when I blabbed to Mom where Dad had hidden his bottle of rye. He had stashed it behind the diapers in the store, hoping no one would find it, especially Mom. He had promised her that he would stop drinking. When I saw him with the bottle of rye, Dad ordered me to keep his hiding place secret. I tried to do it, but when Mom saw me, she noticed a guilty look on my face. She asked what I was hiding. I tried to lie, but she read my mind. She told me that if I didn't tell her what I was hiding, I would be in big trouble. I spilled the beans. Mom went to Dad's hiding place and took away the bottle. Dad was mad at me for a week, and Mom was mad at him for a month.

"You might be right," I said. "They never let me go to anyone's house for dinner. They always want me to come home right after school. It's like they don't want me to have any contact with humans."

"Or maybe they think you'll pick up cooties." Remi grinned.

I scratched my head and laughed. "Too late. I got 'em now."

"You want some more?" Remi grabbed me in a playful headlock and rubbed his knuckles on the top of my head. When he finally let go my hair stood straight up. I licked my palm and patted my hair down. Remi laughed, and I chuckled with him.

Suddenly, he stopped laughing, as an idea gut punched him. "Hey, maybe your mom and dad are on a scouting mission. You know, like when a hockey team sends scouts to the minor leagues to find good players."

"My family wants to recruit aliens?"

"No, they're spying on us. Me. Earthlings.

"But why?"

"Check the magazine. Maybe it says."

The articles all referred to the aliens being curious about Earth, but none said why.

"I guess it's up to us to find out what my parents are doing," I said. "But how?"

Remi cracked a huge grin. "Are you good at spying?"

FIVE

At school, my classmates continued to whisper behind my back. At recess, they asked me nonsense questions like, "if a cat and horse had a baby what would it look like?" or, "what's 23 divided by 17,432 in French?" Trina had told everyone that my brain would smoke out my ears if it was overloaded, and they wanted to push me to the edge.

When I refused to answer, everyone treated me like the lone red sock in a washing machine full of white clothes. But I didn't care. I had a purpose in my life. I was about to set out on a mission to uncover an alien plot with Remi. Fantasies about our adventures replaced all my worries about what the other kids thought of me.

I wanted to share my ideas with Remi, but he told me to ignore him at school. He thought we should act like nothing was out of the ordinary. An Anglais hanging out with a French friend would stand out as unusual. I pretended that I didn't know Remi at all. It wasn't hard since we took classes in different parts of the school.

When the school day ended, I sprinted out of class and headed to the boot room. Trina's freak-a-zoid tour followed me into the schoolyard.

"Keep up with the tour," Trina yelled at the crowd of about ten curious students. "Today, we are going to observe the freak-a-zoid in his natural habitat."

I started to run, and the entire group jogged to keep up with me. When I slowed down, they slowed down too. I turned right, they went right. I went left, they turned left. I was the reluctant leader of a herd of lemmings. I slowed down and shambled toward the chain link fence, trying to figure out how to shake off my followers. Suddenly, an idea sounded off in my brain like a bell ringing. Or was that the bell to dismiss the French students? Either way, I had a plan.

Instead of going home, I doubled back to the school. The Boissonault brothers led other French kids out of the boot room. Perfect. Behind me, Trina's group looped around to follow me. I started to jog; they started to jog. I picked up the pace; they picked up the pace. I broke into a run, and so did they.

I headed for the Boissonault brothers and screamed, "Snowball fight!"

I dove face first into the snow, leaving Trina's charging gang to face Jacques and Jean. The brothers yelled back at their French friends that they were under attack. Trina tried to explain, but she was cut off when a snowball landed smack in the middle of her face. Chaos erupted as the French attacked the Anglais. In the confusion, I crawled through the snow away from the fight and toward home.

In my bedroom, I waited for Remi's signal. I pretended to study to kill time and throw Mom off the scent in case she checked on me. Time crawled to a standstill. I stared at my digital clock and waited for the minute digits to click up. It took 138 seconds for the clock to go from four eleven to four twelve. I suspected my clock was set on alien time.

Finally, I heard a loud thump against the cement wall of my bedroom, followed by another two thumps. I waited. Two thumps, four raps, a dog bark, and seventeen more thumps. That was Remi's signal. I ran to the back of the store and opened the back door to the alley.

"What took you so long?" I asked.

"There was a snowball fight in the schoolyard. I had to help. We totally kicked the Anglais butts. You should have seen the look on their faces."

"Okay, okay," I interrupted. "But an hour of snowball fights?"

"No. I had to go home and get these."

Remi held up a pair of walkie-talkies.

"Cool," I said as he handed one of them to me.

"We have to maintain radio contact at all times," Remi said. "Do you copy?"

"Copy what?"

"Copy is code for understand."

"Why don't you just say 'do you understand'?"

"Because 'copy' sounds cooler. Check your walkie."

I pushed the talk button. Remi's walkie squawked and squealed like an electronic pig. He stepped back.

"What's wrong?" I asked.

"Interference. Just don't stand too close when you're talking into it."

"Copy that."

"Now you're getting it. Okay, ready? Let's go."

Our mission was to get into my parents' bedroom. Remi and I suspected this room possessed all the alien secrets. The trick was to sneak into the room without my parents finding out.

Dad posed no problem. He never left the cash register, so we'd know his location at all times. However, Mom was a rover. Sometimes she cooked in the kitchen. Sometimes she worked in the store. Sometimes she swept the back hall. Keeping tabs on her would prove to be extremely difficult.

We went in search of my mom. Remi and I crept into the main part of the store. I signalled him to move forward along the aisle. He got down on his belly and crawled commando-style. He wormed forward, then froze. He signalled me to stay put. I peeked out and spotted Mom at the front of the store, mopping.

"Do you think she saw us?"

Remi shook his head. "I don't think so. If she moves anywhere near her bedroom, we're done for. Someone has to watch her."

"What does the other guy do?"

"Duh. Search her bedroom," Remi said.

"You go," I said. "I'm too scared."

Remi shook his head. "Chicken."

I didn't argue with him.

"If she starts coming, the code word is jockstrap," Remi instructed.

"Can't I just say she's coming?"

"You want to go in the room?"

"Jockstrap."

"That's better."

"Jockstrap."

"Yes, you've got it right."

"Jockstrap!"

"What are you doing?"

I pointed down the aisle. Mom was coming toward us.

SIX

"Hide!" I pushed Remi toward the living room. We scrambled along the back hall toward the bedrooms. Remi ran into my parents' bedroom before I could stop him.

"Wrong room," I whispered.

Too late. He scrambled under my parents' bed. I had no choice but to squeeze under the bed with him.

"We shouldn't have come in here," I said. "We have to get out."

"Shhh!! I think she's coming."

Mom's footsteps zeroed in on us. I held my breath. Remi froze. We saw Mom's feet in brown slippers. Her toes pointed at us like tiny cameras looking at our nervous faces. My legs quivered. My hands were wet with sweat. I wanted to scream. Instead, I squeezed my walkie-talkie really hard. The sweat made my finger slip and I accidentally pushed the talk button.

SQUAWK!!!!

I panicked and pressed harder. Remi covered his walkie-talkie and glared at me.

"Let go of the button," he mouthed.

I couldn't make out what he was saying.

"Let go of the button," he mouthed again.

I still had no idea what he was saying. Remi pried my finger off the walkie-talking button. The squeal finally stopped. Mom's feet turned to the left and then to the right as she looked around the room for the source of the squawk. It wouldn't be long before she looked under the bed.

Suddenly, an idea hit me.

"Msk. Msk. Msk," I squelched through tight lips. Remi gaped in horror. It looked like I was giving away our hiding spot. I ignored him and kept squelching. He tried to cover my mouth, but I pushed his hand away.

Mom screamed, "Aiya! Mouse."

She ran out the room. Down the hall, she called for Dad to come and kill the mouse under the bed.

"We don't have much time. Let's go." I crawled out from under the bed. Remi followed me.

"What made you think of doing that?" Remi asked.

"Mom hates mice, and our store is full of them."

"Good one, Marty."

I shrugged, pretending I came up with good ideas all the time.

"What do you think she was doing here?" Remi asked.

On top of the pink bed cover, Mom had left a book. It was a black book with strange alien-like markings.

"I think she was after this," I declared.

"Let's take it to your room. We can check it out there."

"Okay. Hurry, before my dad comes."

We raced into my room, closed the door and waited. In the distance, Mom screamed. Then footsteps hurried along the hallway. I cracked the door open slightly and peeked out. Dad ran to the bedroom with a metal mouse trap. Down the hall, Mom told him where to put the trap.

I eased the door closed and propped a chair under the doorknob. Remi plopped on my bed and opened the black book. I looked over his shoulder. The book had strange symbols all over it. Definitely alien in origin. The writing was not English, and Remi said that it didn't look like French either.

"It might be Chinese," he suggested.

"Or it might be alien, disguised as Chinese," I said.

Strange symbols that looked like flattened ants filled the pages. They ran in columns up and down and across.

"Can you read this?" Remi asked.

I shook my head. "It looks like gibberish."

"I'll bet it's your parents' code book. I'll bet it says what the aliens are doing on Earth."

"Yeah, but we can't read it."

"Forget the book," Remi said. "We have to watch your parents. Sooner or later, they're going to slip up, and then we'll find out the truth."

"Copy that."

"Let's rock and roll."

"What?"

"Let's go."

"That another code thing?"

"Yeah. Pretty cool huh?"

I nodded. I took the chair away from the door, and listened for signs of movement. Nothing. I figured Dad went back to the cash register and Mom would not come this way until the mouse was caught. Remi and I crept into the main section of the store. We hid behind the far end of the shelves so that we could spy on my parents. I spotted the top of my dad's bald head behind the cash register. If he was up to anything, we would see it from our vantage point.

For a half an hour, we watched my dad sit at the cash register and read his newspaper. Remi suspected that he was combing the newspaper for information about humans. I agreed. We continued to watch.

David Johnson came in to buy matches. David was Eric Johnson's big brother. The Johnson brothers had the same curly blond hair and dumb sense of humour. However, David liked to kick up more trouble then this kid brother. Rumour had it that he broke all the Rake's car windows, because the Rake suspended him for smoking on school grounds.

David leaned close to my dad and whispered.

"They're passing information to one another," Remi guessed. "We have to hear what they're saying."

I nodded and slunk down the aisle. When I got close enough to hear their conversation, I pretended to "face" some soup cans. "Facing" meant turning cans so that the labels faced front.

"Come on, you can sell me a pack of cigarettes," David whispered.

"You not old enough," my Dad said.

"Look at this face. I'm 30."

Stupidity ran in the Johnson family. David was barely thirteen years old.

"I'll pay double," David offered.

Dad turned him down, "You go before I call your mom and dad."

"Okay, okay. I'm leaving," David said. Then he muttered, "Stupid Chinaman."

My cheeks turned hot and I felt a sting in my eyes. I wiped them and headed back to Remi. I told him that there was no way that David was an alien. He didn't even like my dad. Remi suggested we keep a close eye on Dad for at least another hour, but I didn't feel like spying any more.

"He's not doing a thing," I argued.

"Maybe that's what he wants us to think. Maybe people are supposed to see him just sitting there, so they think nothing is weird."

"Like a decoy."

"Exactly."

"Hold on, hold on. That means my mom is doing all the secret alien stuff."

"Where is she now?" Remi asked.

"I think I heard her near the meat grinder."

"She grinds meat? What kind? Human?"

"I don't know."

"We'd better find out."

In the meat shop, Mom stuffed chunks of meat into the giant silver hamburger grinder. The meat cubes went into a giant tray on top. Then she stuffed the red chunks into the grinder's mouth. Further down the machine, a shower head spit out long strands of hamburger meat. I hoped that the grinder had nothing to do with my parents' master alien plan.

The only way we could spy on Mom was for me to help her grind meat, while Remi hid in the nearby kitchen. He listened to our conversation through the walkie-talkie in my shirt pocket.

I pressed the talk button. "Can you hear me, Remi?"

"Copy that," my pocket answered back. "Actually, I think I can hear you through the door."

Mom turned off the grinder and turned around. "Who you talking to?"

I let go of the walkie button. "No one."

"Go study."

"Okay," I said.

"No," barked my shirt pocket.

"What?" Mom said.

"I meant I'm done," I replied.

"Then take out the garbage."

"Sure," I replied.

My pocket whispered, "Stay there."

I couldn't let Remi down. "Um, Mom. Can I help you make hamburger?"

"You too young to work machine."

"Then can I watch you work?" I asked.

"For a little bit." She shoved chunks of meat into the grinder.

"Why do we have to make hamburger?"

"People like hamburger meat. It's cheap."

"What's it made of?"

"Cows."

I thought of the article about the cow mutilations. I was sure this might have something to do with my parents' mission. They had to grind hamburger meat for their alien brothers and sisters. Maybe aliens liked to barbecue.

"Where do you get the cows?"

"Why you ask so many questions?"

"I'm just curious, Mom."

"You worry about your homework. It better if you not stay here."

"You don't want me here? Where do you want me to be?"

My shirt pocket whispered, "Nice. Ask her about her plans."

I slapped my hand over my pocket.

"Mom, what are your plans for me?"

"What you talk about? You feel okay?"

"I'm fine."

My pocket squawked, "What about the plans?"

She looked at me. "Something is wrong."

Mom stared at me as she started to probe my brain. I filled my mind with weird pictures. A cat in a baby's crib. A fire hydrant rocket ship. Trina dancing with me. Mom moved closer. Her probe increased in power. I started to sweat a little. I blanked out my mind, but all I could think about was Remi. Mom would soon learn everything.

Suddenly, a loud crash in the kitchen distracted her.

"Something is in kitchen," she said.

"I didn't hear anything," I lied.

Another loud clatter came from behind the kitchen door.

"It's the mouse," Mom screamed. "Get your dad!"

"No, let me check it out, Mom." I headed for the door.

Remi yelped. What the heck was he doing back there?

"That is no mouse. Someone is in kitchen," Mom headed to the closed door.

"Run Remi! Run!"

More clattering responded to my yells. Mom raced to the door and swung it open. Remi knelt on the floor, picking up an overturned dish rack and scattered pots and pans.

"What you doing here?" Mom demanded.

"I was doing homework with Marty," Remi lied.

I backed him up. "Yes, I was helping him do math."

"Why you not together then?"

"I was taking a break," I said.

Mom's look showed serious doubt.

"You go home now," she said to Remi.

"But I have to help him," I said.

"Now!"

"I'll see you at school, Marty." Remi scrambled out of the store.

Mom stared after him. I think she tried to read his mind, and whatever she found was not good.

"That boy is trouble," Mom said. "You stay away from him."

She was on to us.

SEVEN

I n my bedroom, I pretended to read my Hardy Boys book, but I kept thinking about Remi. I squished my ear against the wall, hoping to hear his secret signal. Silence greeted me. He was not coming back tonight. I would have to wait until the morning to tell him about my mom being on to us.

Tomorrow couldn't come fast enough. I wanted to talk to Remi right now. I felt like one of the Hardy Boys, and I had just been separated from my detective partner. I wanted the writer to devise an easy way for me to reach Remi. But this was real life, not a book. I jumped off the bed and paced around the room, trying to figure out a plan.

Finally, it hit me. I could sneak out of the store, follow Remi's footprints in the snow until I reached his house. Then the two of us could hide out in his room and plan our next step. I got dressed and rushed to the back of the store so that I could pick up Remi's trail.

Mom stood guard at the back door with a broom and a bunch of questions. I suspected she had picked up my thoughts and intercepted me before I could take off. I tried to empty my brain of all thoughts of Remi and aliens.

"What you doing?" she asked.

"I'm looking for my pen," I lied.

"Why you wear your winter jacket?"

"I think I lost the pen outside."

"How you lose it out there?"

I shrugged, "I guess I was clumsy. I'm going to look for it."

She shook her head. "You get pen from Dad."

"But it was my lucky pen. I should try to find it at least."

She shook her head. "It too dark outside. You not find it tonight."

Thinking fast, I blurted out, "I can't take a new pen. We'll lose money from a sale."

"You right," she agreed. Then she tossed me the broom. "You work for it. Sweep the front."

My clever alien mom wanted me near Dad so that he could keep an eye on me. I thought that I could wait. Sooner or later, Mom would leave her back door post and I would be able to slip out.

"Give me your jacket and boots," she said.

Without my winter gear, I'd never survive outside. Mom knew this, and she knew that I knew this, and I knew that she knew. She had read my mind and thwarted yet another one of my plans. I ripped off my winter coat and kicked off my boots, then I stomped to the front of the store with the broom.

"Don't make so much noise," she barked.

I stepped quietly, but I took my time getting to the front. I stopped often to sweep tiny specks of dust or face some cans. All the while, I peeked back at Mom, who continued to stand guard over my escape route.

I doubted that I would be able to get to Remi's house tonight. As I shuffled to the front, I wondered about Remi's home. Was it attached to a shop or was it a real house? Did he have normal human parents? I suspected he had all the things that I had ever wanted in a home. I imagined his parents hugging him when he came home, and everyone in the house sitting down together for dinner. In my mind, they all seemed like such a family. I wished I lived in a place like that.

The truth hit me; there was such a place — my home planet. I wondered if my real home existed in this galaxy. I wished that I came from Saturn. I liked the planet's rainbow-coloured rings. I imagined that on Saturn aliens didn't have to wear disguises. On

Saturn, we all looked the same. On Saturn, no one got picked on.

I wondered what I really looked like. Maybe I had rings around my head, like my planet. Perhaps I could hang stuff off the rings. Or better yet, I had four giant gorilla arms and I could lift giant meteorites or move Saturnian mountains. I imagined having three heads so that I could read more than one book at the same time. I had mega-powerful eyes, so that I never needed glasses. I had super-selective hearing so that I could only hear the nice things that people said about me.

However, all this thinking about Saturn saddened me. I realized that I did not live on that really cool planet. Instead, I suffered on a strange world where everyone looked and acted different. Why couldn't Mom and Dad stay on Saturn? What was so important about Bouvier that we had to live here? Why didn't my parents ask me if I wanted to live on Earth? I wanted to expose them as aliens so that we would be forced to return to Saturn. But without evidence, my chance of success was as far away as my home world.

When I reached the cash register, I noticed Dad talking to a tall, thin grey-haired man, who looked about a hundred years old. What really set him apart were his black clothes. The only white in his dark outfit was a bit of his collar, which barely peeked out from under his black overcoat.

Was Dad talking to a Night Watchman?

Stunned, I dropped my broom. The two men glanced at me. I snatched the broom and looked away. Then I pretended to find dirt under the chocolate bar rack. I swept the tiled floor as I eavesdropped on the two men.

"It's settled. If all goes well, they should be here within two weeks," the Night Watchman whispered. He had a really raspy voice and a French accent.

My dad said, "I think they will be very happy here."

"Anywhere is better than where they came from. Poor souls."

"Do you think they will have trouble fitting in?"

"I'm hoping that you will show them how to integrate."

Integrate? What did that mean? I tried to remember the definition. I broke the word in half. "Inte" was like "enter." "Grate" was like "great." It was "great" to "enter"? Integrate meant that the aliens thought it was great to enter the human race.

"I will take good care of them," Dad promised.

"That's why I picked you. How much for the milk?"

Dad shook his head. "No charge. Take it."

"Bless you, George," the Night Watchman murmured. He picked up his carton of milk and left the store.

I positioned myself by the window to spy on the departing Night Watchman. The first big break in the alien case made me so excited that I didn't see Dad come up behind me.

"Marty, get back to work. Sweep in the back."

I stalled, "Mom told me to work here."

"Then you should work," he ordered.

Dad ushered me away from the window. I lost sight of the Night Watchman, but it didn't matter. I knew the master plan. Aliens were on their way to Earth.

EIGHT

"It has to be an invasion," blurted Remi. He leaned against the pedestal of the giant statue of Jesus Christ to prop himself up. The towering stone Jesus held out his hands to embrace all the people in the schoolyard.

Remi noticed some nearby English guys and muttered, "People are looking."

I strolled to the statue's back side so that we didn't look like we were talking to each other. Remi and I looked weird talking to the granite statue, but it was better than being seen together.

"It sounded like the Night Watchman was behind it all," I said to Jesus' heels.

"I knew it was an invasion. I mean I didn't want to tell you because I didn't want you to freak out. But deep down, I knew aliens were coming to invade Earth."

"Why would they — we — the aliens be interested in taking over the planet?"

"I saw this in a movie last summer. It's because they need slaves to do all their work."

"Really?"

"Yeah. Your parents are scouts," Remi said to Jesus' toes. "They want to see how much of a fight we'll put up. And so far we haven't put up any. They think we're easy targets. That's why they're sending more aliens."

"Do you know the weird thing about the Night Watchman? He didn't look like my parents. He looked more like the Rake."

"Our principal is an alien too?"

"No, I meant, the Night Watchman looked human. I don't think he was an alien."

"Let me think," Remi said.

The other kids noticed Remi and I talking to Jesus' feet and giggled.

"We should move," I suggested.

As Remi came around the statue, he whispered out the side of his mouth, "Boot room."

He sauntered toward the school. I waited for a minute, then I meandered a wide arc that eventually led to the boot room. Inside, Remi pretended to fix his snow pants. I started to take off my boots. I hopped around on one foot, a little off balanced, and bumped into Remi. He pushed me away and I slammed into the wall

"Stop fooling around, Marty," Remi barked. "I think I figured it out."

I stopped hopping.

"The Night Watchman is an Earthling who's turned against the humans. He's a traitor."

"Why would he do that?" I asked.

"Maybe they offered him something."

"My dad didn't charge him for the milk," I suggested.

"Free stuff. That could be it."

"You'd turn over the entire human race for a carton of milk?" I asked.

"Chocolate milk?"

He made a good point. Everyone had a price.

"He's preparing for the invasion," Remi said.

"We have to stop him."

"Yeah, the aliens picked the wrong planet. We're gonna kick their alien butts."

"Hey, I have an alien butt."

"Yeah, well, you're gonna have to decide whose side you're on."

"Can't you leave me out of it?" I asked.

Remi threw me a puzzled look.

I explained, "It's just that I don't know if I can stand up to my parents."

"You're either with Earth or against Earth."

"But I don't want to upset my mom or dad."

A few kids ran into the boot room. Remi cut off all communications. He stormed outside.

Remi's statement made me think of the French/English war in the schoolyard. Only this time, the French and English would unite as human beings against aliens. I had to choose between my parents and the Earthlings. I was torn.

I stepped into my boots and headed outside, where Remi waited for my answer. I couldn't let my friend down.

I walked past him and whispered, "I'm on your side."

Remi grunted, "Good. Follow me."

He ran to the giant snow hill near the statue of Jesus. I scanned the schoolyard for any spies, then I followed him.

On the other side of the hill, away from curious eyes, Remi patted me on the back. "I knew you'd see things the right way, Marty. We're going to win this war."

"I don't want to hurt my parents."

"We won't. We're just gonna scare them into thinking that an invasion would be a bad idea. A very bad idea."

"But they're not the ones planning it. I think the Night Watchman is the leader."

"Then we have to get to him. Did you see where he went?"

"Yes, he went out of the store."

"And?"

"My dad grabbed me before I could see where he went."

"What did the guy look like?"

"He had grey hair. And he was tall. He had a hat. And he was old."

Remi guessed, "How old? Like thirty?"

"Maybe more."

Remi said, "It's safe to say that he's not at school."

"Why?"

"You would have recognized him."

I thought only the Hardy Boys were capable of brilliant ideas.

"So that leaves the rest of the town," he said.

"Not quite. Just the men." I wanted to impress Remi with my deductive powers.

"So where can you find a lot of grey-haired men?"

Remi smiled smugly like he knew the answer. I didn't want to look dumb, so I took a wild guess. "The barbershop?"

Remi's grin deflated. "How did you know?"

Maybe I could read minds like Mom. I wasn't sure. I shrugged.

"Doesn't matter," Remi said. "The barbershop is where all the old farmers go to tell stories."

"But none of them wear black," I said. "It's more like plaid. And they wear green farmer hats."

"They have grey hair," Remi snapped. "You got any better ideas."

Remi seemed cranky. Instead of poking holes in his theory, I said, "You're right. We should check it out."

Remi didn't answer.

"I said we should check it out. Why aren't you answering me?"

Remi roared and threw me into the snow bank. He pounced on my back and pushed my head down. I got a mouth full of snow. I tried to push up, but he held me down.

"Dumb Anglais. You're spying on us," Remi shouted. "Don't worry fellas, I got this one under control."

Through my snow-filled ears I could hear boys laugh and walk away. After what seemed like forever, Remi pulled me up. Snow caked on my glasses. I wiped them clean, while Remi brushed the snow off my jacket.

"What was that about?" I asked.

Remi cocked his head toward the schoolyard. The Boissonault brothers walked away. "If they saw us together, I'd be in big trouble."

"Couldn't you pretend that you didn't know me?"

"All Anglais get face washes if they're caught alone. That's the rule of war."

"You could have warned me before you stuck my face in the snow," I pouted.

"I could let Jean and Jacques finish the job," Remi offered. "Hey guys!"

I clamped my hand over his mouth. "Don't even think about doing that."

Remi laughed as he tried to get free of my hand and call for the Boissonaults.

"I thought you were my friend," I said.

He stopped laughing. "I am, but not at school. The Boissonaults would kill me if they saw us together."

"So you're going to give me a face wash every time you see me at school?"

"I was doing you a favour. Jacques is pretty mean when it comes to snow washes. The last kid got eight stitches."

"Gee, thanks. Not."

"Do you think you're the only one scared of being beat up?"

"But you're really tough."

"There's only one of me," he confessed. "And there are two of them. This one time, Denis Aquin tried to trade hockey cards with Ray Blinston. Jacques and Jean caught them by the soccer goal posts. They hammered Denis pretty good. He didn't come to school for three days."

"I thought French guys stuck together," I said.

"The Anglais aren't much better. I heard they made Ray eat his hockey cards."

I remembered Ray puked up paper during our math test. I thought he had swallowed a cheat sheet, but now I knew where the paper came from. Even though they claimed to be different, the English and the French boys in my school did have one thing in common. They were all jerks.

Remi continued, "If anyone found out about you and me, we'd get it bad. Real bad. Do you want that?"

I thought about how awful my U.F.O. magazine would taste. "No."

"That's why we have to make sure no one sees us together," Remi said.

I agreed.

Remi turned around to locate Jean and Jacques in case they doubled back, as they were known to do. Suddenly, I had a wicked idea. I scooped a handful of snow, snuck up behind Remi, and gave him a face wash.

"What was that for?" he sputtered.

"I thought Eric Johnson was looking this way. I have to protect myself too."

I cracked a grin. Remi scowled for a minute, then broke into a big grin.

Remi spit out some snow and said, "Okay, we're even."

I playfully punched his arm to seal the deal. He punched my arm back, hard. I made a mental note not to play punch buggy with him in the future.

"So after school, we start looking for the Night Watchman," I said.

He nodded. "We'd better get to class. Don't want to get detention."

I agreed. I ran to the building, while Remi hung back. A snowball pelted the back of my head. I whipped around. Remi whistled, pretending nothing happened. I knew he threw the snowball and I promised to get even with him later.

Fridays usually dragged on because they were the last day before the weekend, but this Friday went by especially slow. I glanced at the clock about a thousand times. I looked like I had a nervous tic, because my head kept twisting to see the clock. Trina made fun of me, and said that my brain had short-circuited.

Everyone ignored her. Trina lost her popularity when she led the freak-a-zoid tour into an unintentional snowball fight with the French. She slumped in her desk and pouted. Her silence sounded so sweet.

Finally, the bell rang to end the day. In such a rush to start my mission, I nearly forgot to take my homework. I had to run back and get it. Mrs. Connor scolded me for running in school and warned me to take it slow. I barely heard her as I sprinted out of the classroom.

Outside, I headed to the far end of the schoolyard where Remi and I had agreed to meet. I hid in the bare bushes, but quickly noticed that the leafless twigs offered no camouflage. A trio of grade two girls snickered as they walked passed me. The bell rang to dismiss the French kids. More students gawked at me as they headed out of the schoolyard. I needed a new hiding place. I walked out from behind the bushes and walked along the fence to an isolated spot. Then I laid flat on my back in the snow and melted into the snow drift. I searched the blue sky for Saturn. I stared so hard that little dots formed in my field of vision. I let them dance around the sky and tried to make them form my home world. They just gave me a headache after a while.

I sat up. The schoolyard was deserted. Had I missed Remi, or did I mix up our meeting place? Maybe he told me to meet him in the school. I trudged through the snow back to the two-story brick building.

Suddenly, Remi came around the corner. I waved to him, but he shook his head. I put my hand down. As he got closer, I noticed that Remi's jacket was ripped and he had a black eye.

"What happened?" I asked.

He walked right past me. He whispered, "Are they following me?"

I peeked around the corner of the school and spotted Eric Johnson with six stocky Anglais boys. Eric danced around, using a piece of Remi's jacket like a belly dancer's veil. His friends laughed. I crept away from my hiding spot and ran to Remi, who had made it to the fence. He tried to piece his torn jacket together.

"Did Eric's friends do that?" I asked.

"Duh."

"Why did they do that to you?"

"Why do you think monkey butt? I'm French and they're not."

"Didn't your friends come to help?"

"No, I was waiting until everyone was gone."

"I'm sorry, Remi."

"They said it was for the snowball fight that happened the other day. It wasn't your fault."

My stomach knotted up. I had started the fight when I tried to shake off Trina's freak-a-zoid tour.

"Are you going to be okay?" I asked.

"I get worse when I play hockey," Remi mumbled through his fat lip.

I said nothing as Remi tromped up the street. Until now, the French/English war was a stupid battle between guys I didn't like. But now it claimed Remi as a casualty, and I played a big part in it. I watched my friend limp up the street. I couldn't stand it.

I ran up to him and confessed, "Remi, it's my fault. Trina's tour group was following me. I had to lose them so that I could meet you. I tricked them into charging at the Boissonault brothers. That's what started the snowball fight. It's because of me that Eric and his jerks attacked you. I didn't think they would go that far."

Remi growled, "Why do you think we call it a war? One day, the Anglais get one of us. The next, the Boissonaults get one of you. Well not you. But them. You know what I mean."

"I'm sorry," I said.

Remi went sulky silent. I tried to get him to yell at me, but he refused to say anything. I apologized a thousand times, but he just glared at me. I tried to change the subject. "So do you know what else I found out about the Night Watchman?"

Remi didn't speak.

"I think he's French."

Remi looked at me. "You think the French are traitors?"

"No, I'm just saying the guy spoke English, but with a French accent."

"Why would a French man work with aliens?"

"The aliens probably thought the Anglais were too dumb to work with," I said.

Remi laughed. "You got that right."

I cracked jokes about the Anglais and how stupid they were. They brightened his mood. I told more Anglais jokes. By the time we reached the barbershop, Remi was in a good mood. He even noted, "You sure know a lot of jokes about the Anglais."

I nodded. "I guess I was saving them up."

Remi tried to peer through the barbershop window, but the icy windows blocked our view.

"There's no way we can see inside," Remi sighed.

A bold idea hit me. "Come on. I've got a plan."

I walked straight into the barbershop. Warm air blasted against my face and the strong smell of old socks mixed with bleach squirreled up my nose. Like everything else in Bouvier, the shop was small. A red vinyl chair sat in the centre of the room, which meant the barber could only work on one customer at a time. Customers sat and waited on one of two benches against a wall. Between the benches, magazines sprawled across a shaky end table.

Tom, the bald shop owner, trimmed an older man's brown bangs. On the bench, two old farmers wore John Deere farmer caps. We couldn't see the colour of their hair.

"Hello, boys," Tom smiled, revealing a missing front tooth. "Take a seat. I'll get to you in a snip. Get it? Snip. Barber. Snip."

The farmers chuckled at Tom's joke. I nudged Remi and laughed.

"Actually, it's my friend who needs the haircut," I said.

"No I don't."

I jabbed Remi in the ribs to shut him up.

"He's scared," I said.

"No need to worry. I don't bite. But I just might nip your ear off. Ha, ha."

One of the farmers leaned forward and whispered, "Why do you think Frank and I wear hats now?"

Remi's eyes widened. Everyone in the room burst out laughing. I ushered Remi to the other bench and sat down, while the old guys continued talking to Tom about the good old days.

Remi whispered, "This is your plan?"

"Relax. There are two people ahead of you. This will give us time to see if the Night Watchman shows up."

"I'm not letting Tom touch my hair. I heard he's so bad at cutting that his own hair won't grow because it's scared he might try to cut it."

"Trust me, Remi."

I leaned back and listened to the old guys complain about how candy bars used to cost three cents, but now were too expensive. Tom said he hadn't changed the price of his haircuts in twenty years. The farmers joked that he hadn't change the style of his haircuts either.

Remi fidgeted beside me. Then, the door swung open and blew cold air inside. A man in a heavy black overcoat, black shoes, a black scarf, and a black toque entered. He spun around to a coat rack and unwrapped his scarf. What luck! We had found the Night Watchman on our first try.

"Hey, Greg," Tom called out.

The man hung up his scarf and took off his hat to reveal a full head of blond hair. Then he turned around and greeted Tom. He looked much younger than the real Night Watchman.

"Dad, I left you last week and you were working on Eddie's hair. Is it taking you that long these days?"

Everyone chuckled. The farmers launched into a conversation with Greg, interested in his progress at university. Greg told them he was now studying to be a doctor, but whined that text books had become very expensive. This renewed the farmers' complaints about how chocolate bars used to cost three cents.

The conversation paused when Tom finished Eddie's haircut. Eddie climbed out of the red chair and thanked Tom for a great job. His head looked lopsided, but I didn't say a thing. Eddie waved to the farmers and left the barbershop.

"Okay, you're next son," Tom said and pointed his scissors at Remi.

Remi's mouth dropped open. He motioned to the farmers. "What about them?"

Frank chuckled, "We're just here for the atmosphere."

"I changed my mind," Remi squawked.

Greg laughed, "Hey Dad, it looks like your reputation precedes you."

The farmers laughed, but Tom scowled at his son.

Tom clucked at Remi. "Young fella, by the time I'm done, you'll have to beat off the girls with a stick."

"I don't like girls," Remi protested.

This ignited more laughs.

"They might know who the Night Watchman is," I whispered. "We have to get them to talk."

Remi didn't budge from the bench. Meanwhile, Tom swept Eddie's hair off the chair. Greg sat down beside the farmers and complained about how broke he was.

I interrupted him. "The style of the coats these days. Long black jackets. Don't see many of them around do you?"

Greg shot me an evil look, but the farmers listed the people who had black coats, while Tom put Remi in the vinyl chair and attached the apron around his neck. The men argued about how dark navy blue was not black. I tried to divide the list into black coats and navy blue coats. Tom claimed that overcoats would never be as warm as down-filled vests. Frank said vests made him look fat.

"If you want to find people with black jackets, just hang out at the IGA," a frustrated Greg spat. "Everyone shops there now. Who would shop at the Chinaman's?"

Everyone stopped talking. Tom glared at his son.

"I like to get my meat from your dad," Tom grabbed a water bottle and sprayed Remi's hair.

The farmers launched into a discussion about the best cuts of meat. Tom liked boneless strip loins. The farmers enjoyed T-bones, because they liked to gnaw off the gristle. Tom carelessly waved his scissors around and said bones were for dogs. Then he grabbed a handful of Remi's bangs and snipped.

Remi yelped and hopped out of the chair. He ripped off his apron, grabbed his jacket and bolted out of the barbershop. The farmers laughed, while Tom shook his head.

"I knew I should have put a seat belt in the chair," he said.

Everyone laughed. I grabbed my jacket as Greg started talking again about his financial problems. I hoped Tom wouldn't give his son any money.

Outside, Remi paced back and forth in front of the frosted window.

"Look at what he did." Remi showed me his trimmed bangs. They reminded me of Tom's uneven smile.

"It's not that bad," I lied.

"That was a dumb idea. We didn't find out anything."

"Wrong. I learned all the information we need."

"What do you mean? Do you know who the Night Watchman is?"

"No, but I know where to look for him."

NINE

While my parents' store sat deserted on Saturdays, the IGA teemed with more people than a toy store at Christmas. Customers jammed the wide aisles with their overfull shopping carts. Pony-tailed cashiers rang up groceries. The jolly store manager directed traffic and handed out coupons. Scrawny stock boys carried out groceries for an endless line of customers. Sooner or later the Night Watchman had to make his appearance in the store.

"Why wouldn't he buy his groceries at your parents' store?" Remi asked. "He got his milk there."

I said, "It would look suspicious if only shopped there. Besides, he has to keep his eye on everyone else."

Remi agreed with my logic. "So he's like a spy."

"Yeah. My parents spied on the people who shopped at their store, but now that the IGA is open, they need another spy."

"Why don't they do it themselves?"

"Think about it Remi. It would look pretty odd if the owners of the competition shopped here."

"I didn't think of it that way."

"Grab a cart and we'll pretend to shop," I ordered.

We filled our cart with cookies, chips, pop, cans of stew, and toilet paper – just about everything in the store. We didn't plan on buying any of the groceries. We just wanted to blend in with the other shoppers so that we could spy on them.

Mostly women shopped in the store. It was hard to spot any men, let alone the Night Watchman. Still, Remi and I circled the store and tossed random groceries into our cart. By our fifth time past the sweet pickles, a stock boy became suspicious. He stopped facing the pickles we had just walked by and followed us. Remi and I tried to look casual as we jammed more groceries into the few remaining spaces of our overfull cart.

"Need help finding stuff?" the pimply-faced teenager squawked.

"We're fine," I replied.

"Yeah," Remi chimed in.

"Are you shopping for your family?"

We nodded.

"So you're brothers?"

"Yup," Remi answered. He glanced at me. "Nope. Maybe."

The stock boy crossed his arms, waiting for Remi to settle on an answer.

I jumped in quickly, "I'm adopted."

"Yeah," said Remi. "So if you don't mind, we have to finish shopping."

"I suppose these feminine pads are for one of you?" We nodded.

"What do you use them for?" the stock boy asked.

"Duh," said Remi. "If you don't know, why should we tell you?"

"Call me curious." He held up the pink package.

"Well," I said. "They're for the bathroom."

I remembered seeing the same package in the bathroom, and I knew that Mom used them, but not all the time. They were special. But what were they for?

"Come on. What do you do with them?" The stock boy snapped.

"Uh, when your face gets really dirty, so dirty that a normal face cloth won't clean it, you use the pads to wipe the grime off."

The stock boy laughed. "Not even close."

Remi shot back, "Oh yeah? Do you know what you use them for?"

"Uh, well, they're, it's kinda like . . . hey, you guys aren't buying groceries. You're just fooling around!"

I turned to Remi and yelled, "Run!"

He bolted down the aisle, while I shoved the cart over the stock boy's foot. I zigzagged down the aisle, dodging impatient shoppers. The angry teenager yelled after us. We ignored him. As we rounded the corner, a stock girl near the meat cooler cut us off. Hearing her co-worker's call for help, she grabbed Remi and me by the back of our shirts. She hauled us down the aisle to the limping stock boy. He thanked her and told her he could handle things from here.

"Okay, that's enough fooling around," he said. "I know you're not buying any of these groceries. Put it all back where you found it."

We claimed to be serious about shopping, but we shut up when he threatened to call our parents. Remi and I mumbled our apologies and pushed the cart down the aisle. We took our time returning the items to their rightful places so that we could still spy on the shoppers.

By the time our cart was empty, it seemed like everyone in town had passed through the store except the Night Watchman. Remi and I left the store without a single lead.

"He's got to be in town somewhere," I said.

"We'll find him if it takes all day. Well, as long as we finish before six."

"What happens at six? Do you turn into a pumpkin?" I joked.

"Duh! Hockey Night in Canada is on."

"So?"

"The Leafs are playing."

"Who cares about the Leafs at a time like this?"

Remi punched me in the arm so hard that I thought his fist went out the other side. "Never, ever, say that again."

I rubbed my sore arm. "Okay, okay. We'll quit so you can see the hockey game."

"You sure you didn't dream up this guy?"

"He's real," I argued. "He's got to be in town. He can't hide forever."

"Maybe he beamed up to a space ship," Remi suggested.

"He's not an alien. He's a human, and he'll show up sooner or later."

"We could watch Main Street. Everyone walks down Main Street on Saturdays."

"That's a good idea."

Remi tapped the side of his head and claimed, "Not just for cracking walnuts."

"Huh?"

"Just keep your eyes open," Remi said.

Very soon however, we discovered the fatal flaw in Remi's plan. Main Street offered no shelter from the icy winter wind. We stomped our feet to pound feeling into them, and we hugged ourselves to make sure our arms didn't go numb. All the while, no one resembling the Night Watchman walked down the block.

When the sun started to set, Remi began to fidget and check his watch. He wanted to give up for the day, but I told him that Hockey Night in Canada wasn't starting for another two hours. However, the crowd dwindled and still no Night Watchman.

Suddenly, Remi cried out. He pointed to the Sears outlet store. A man in a long black jacket stepped out of the shop. I didn't get a good look at his face, but I it might have been him. We chased after the man, until I saw his white sneakers. As we got closer, I also noticed he stood much shorter than the Night Watchman. Remi and I let this guy go.

"There's another one," Remi shouted.

Another man in a black overcoat left the Sears outlet. He was too big. Another man stepped out of the store. He was too young. I started to feel like Goldilocks looking for just the right bowl of porridge.

"Maybe they're all Night Watchmen," Remi suggested.

The Sears outlet seemed to have more than its fair share of men in long black jackets, but what did a clothing store have to do with alien invasions? I had to know. I crept closer. In the shop's display window, a mannequin dressed in a long black jacket stood beside a discount sign. We were getting nowhere with our investigation, and Remi wanted to get home to see his game.

"We're not gonna to find the Night Watchman today," he complained.

"I guess we can try again tomorrow."

"Good idea. We'll start fresh. Do you want to come over to my place and watch the hockey game?"

No one had ever asked me over to their house. I was thrilled at the idea of watching television at Remi's place. Maybe his mom would let me eat popcorn or put my feet up on the couch.

"I have to ask my parents first," I said.

"Give me a call when you find out."

Remi rattled off his phone number and headed down the street. I tried to replay the number in my mind, but he spoke too fast. I called after him to tell me his number again. What I saw choked the words out of my mouth.

The Night Watchman walked on the other side of the street. Not only did he have black clothes, but he also had grey hair. I ran after Remi and grabbed his jacket.

"Hey, watch it! My jacket's ripped enough already."

"I think it's him," I whispered.

"Who?"

"Him." I pointed at the Night Watchman across the street. I saw his face. He was definitely the man who talked to my dad about the alien invasion.

"We have to follow him," I blurted out.

"But the hockey game is about to start."

"What's more important? The safety of the planet or a Leafs' game?"

Before he could answer, I pushed Remi after the Night Watchman.

"He looks familiar," he said as we jogged behind the old man.

"Duh." I finally got a chance to use Remi's comeback. "I described him to you."

"Watch it, monkey butt," he warned.

"Maybe you saw him at one of your hockey games."

"No, but I'm pretty sure I've seen him before," Remi said. "I gotta get a better look at his face."

The Night Watchman walked to the giant brick church. He took out keys and opened the huge wooden cathedral doors. He glanced back before he stepped inside, giving us a clear view of his face.

"I know who that is," Remi blurted.

"No way. Who is he?"

"That's Father Sasseville."

"Who?"

"The priest!"

TEN

"What does a priest have to do with aliens?" I said.

"I don't know," Remi said, stumped. "Okay, if we break this down, we can figure it out. What does Father Sasseville do? "

"Well, he runs the church. Sometimes, he reads from the Bible. Sometimes, he says mass. And sometimes he talks about the good things that Jesus Christ does?"

"Jesus? You mean the statue guy in the schoolyard?"

"Yeah."

I shook my head. "I just thought he was the first principal at the school."

"For a guy who reads a lot, you sure don't know much," he joked.

"Okay, Mr. Smarty Pants," I said. "Why don't you tell me?"

"Jesus is the holiest of the holy. He's our saviour. When he was born, three wise men came to see him. And they gave him all sorts of cool stuff."

"Video games?"

"No, it was in the old days. They gave him gold, frankincense and myrrh."

"What are frankincense and myrrh?"

"I have no idea," Remi said. "But they're probably as valuable as gold. Anyway, a star led the wise men to where Jesus was born. They said the star was a sign that he was gonna be someone great."

"A star?"

"Yeah, you know. The little lights in the sky. It flew across the sky."

"You mean like a U.F.O.?"

Remi's mouth dropped open as he made the connection.

I kept going. "Maybe myrrh is milk."

Remi flashed me a puzzled look

"My dad gave the Night Watchman some milk."

"What could be so important about free milk?" Remi asked.

"Cows!"

"The mutilations? Maybe aliens need milk to live. It's like air to them."

"Then why did my dad give away his milk to Father Sasseville?"

"I don't know. Maybe to show him how much the aliens trust him."

"That's stupid. My mom could read his mind and find out if he could be trusted or not."

"Yeah, I didn't think of that. Hey, can you read minds? What am I thinking right now?"

I closed my eyes and tried to reach into Remi's brain. I found nothing. I opened my eyes and shook my head.

"Too bad," Remi sighed. "It would have come in handy to figure out what your parents are up to."

"I guess we'll have to figure it out for ourselves," I said.

"There's got to be some kind of link between aliens cows, milk and Father Sasseville. I just don't see what it is yet."

"I'll bet the priest knows," I offered.

"Yeah, but how are we going to find out?"

"Ask him?" I joked.

"Good idea!"

The next thing I knew, Remi and I sat in Father Sasseville's office. Behind the priest, high up on his wall, a giant cross with Jesus looked down on us, just like the statue in the schoolyard. Beside me, Remi held his black toque in his hands as if he were praying.

"What can I do for you, my sons?"

Remi leaned forward and whispered, "My friend wants to join the Church."

Father Sasseville leaned back in his creaky chair and smiled at me. "You're making a good decision."

"I'd like to learn more about your religion first," I blurted.

Remi elbowed me. "He means he wants to get more information so he can fit in with the rest of us."

Father Sasseville beamed. "I know just what you need."

He pulled open the top drawer of his desk and took out a black book. Was everything he owned black?

"This is all you need to get started," he said. "The Good Book."

He handed me the thick book. As I flipped through it, I squinted at the tiny print. I would need weeks to read this book.

"Thanks," I said. "But I have some questions that can't wait."

"Yes, my son. What answers do you seek?"

"What do you know about things that come from the sky?" I asked.

Father Sasseville flashed a curious look at Remi. His raspy voice cracked a bit as he asked, "What have you been telling this young man?"

Remi looked more nervous than I had ever seen him before. He might as well have been talking to the Boissonault brothers. "I told him about the baby Jesus and the wise men."

I peeked at Father Sasseville for a reaction, but he just leaned back in his leather chair and drummed his fingers against his lips. I went on the offensive, hoping to catch him off guard.

"I know about the star," I said.

"Ah, yes, the guiding light," Father Sasseville said without hesitation.

"Why did it move?" Remi asked. The two of us worked together like the Frank and Joe Hardy. I was Frank, the smart one.

"It is a mystery and a miracle," Father Sasseville answered.

When we heard "mystery," Remi and I gave each other knowing looks.

I interrogated Father Sasseville, "Did the light move like a U.F.O.?"

"I never thought of it that way, but if it makes it easier to understand the story, then yes."

We had our man.

I turned to the priest. "So why would this star guide the wise men to the baby? What was in it for the star?"

"I don't understand your question my son."

Remi jumped in. "What he means is why did the star do all this?"

"Excuse me?"

"Was it to take over the world?" I stared into the priest's blue eyes.

"What?"

Remi lost his nerve and looked down at his shoes.

"Maybe we should start you in Catechism Class. And Remi, you might need a refresher too. Why don't we start with that?"

"But I need answers now," I said.

"At times, eagerness can be a hindrance and patience a virtue."

"What?" I said.

"Don't be so quick to forge ahead. The joy is the journey, not the destination."

I perked up. "What kind of journey? Where do you want to go?"

"It's an expression, my son," Father Sasseville sighed. "Perhaps you should start reading the Bible. If it doesn't give you the answers, then come back and we will talk some more."

I examined the heavy black book in my hands. Father Sasseville was stalling. I lobbed one more question at him.

"What was so important about the baby?"

"Christ is our saviour. We owe everything to this child."

Suddenly, the answer cut through the fog like a lighthouse beacon. I nudged Remi. Time to go.

"Thanks Father," he said. You've helped us a lot. I'll make sure Marty reads the book."

"Yes, thank you, sir," I said.

"Tell your father I said hello," Father Sasseville said, looking me square in the eyes.

I stammered, "Sure."

I felt like I was standing on thin ice. I knew the ice would soon crack and I would fall in. I didn't know when, but I knew it was going to be pretty quick and cold. I scrambled out of Father Sasseville's office. Once Remi and I were outside the church, I sprinted down the street. I wanted to put as much distance between the Night Watchman and myself. Remi chased after me. Two blocks away, I slowed to a walk.

"What was the rush?" Remi asked.

"I know why the Night Watchman is Father Sasseville, and why the Church is tied up with the aliens."

"Why?"

"Jesus was an alien."

"No way. You're crazy."

"Listen," I said. "The U.F.O. led the humans to this baby, right? Why would it do that? Because Jesus is from outer space!"

Remi shook his head in disbelief.

"That's why his statue is high up and looking down at us. He's really an alien in disguise."

"Jesus doesn't look anything like you or your parents. He looks more like my dad."

"Maybe it's a different kind of disguise," I said.

Remi shook his head, "If the aliens could disguise themselves to look like Earthlings, why would your family look Chinese? It just doesn't make sense. Think about it. You could have blended in with the rest of us. You could invade Earth and no one would know. Why would your parents disguise themselves as Chinese if they could look like Jesus?"

I couldn't argue against Remi. If I was an invading alien and I could pick my disguise, I definitely would not pick the one I had now.

Remi continued, "Besides, Jesus teaches us to accept people for who they are. He doesn't talk about alien invasions. He talks about harmony and peace."

"Really?"

"Yeah."

"But maybe harmony and peace are codes for alien invasion."

Remi sighed, "Do you really think that?"

"No, but if he's not an alien, what's his connection to the U.F.O.?"

Remi offered a theory. "Maybe the aliens found him because they knew he wouldn't judge them. He'd accepted everyone. And he would accept aliens. That's why they wanted him to be the king of kings."

I hated to admit it, but Remi's explanation sounded pretty good, except for one thing.

"Not enough people listened to him," I said. "There's still war in the world. And some people still don't like people who look different."

"Yeah," Remi said. "But it's not his fault that some people don't listen."

"Maybe the aliens can't wait for Earthlings to accept them. That's why they've decided to invade."

"Why would Father Sasseville help?" Remi asked.

"I don't know," I said. "Maybe the aliens have some kind of mind control."

Remi gasped. "Can you do that?"

"No, I tried to make Eric Johnson pick his nose in class the other day, but he didn't do it."

"Maybe his brain was too small."

"Remi, this is no time for jokes," I said. "We have to stop the alien invasion. We have to get help."

"From who?"

I had no idea.

ELEVEN

Remi and I had to tell someone about the alien invasion, but we didn't know who to trust. I worried that my alien parents controlled more people than Father Sasseville. Remi believed that if they controlled a priest, they might also control members of his church.

"We have to look for people who aren't at church on Sunday morning," I said.

"Why?"

"They're probably the only ones who haven't been turned into puppets."

Remi asked, "Do you think your parents control everybody's minds?"

"I don't know, but we can't take any chances. If we talk to anyone who goes to church, they might tell Father Sasseville, and then my parents will know everything."

"You're right," Remi said. He glanced around the street to see if anyone was eavesdropping.

"We have to find rebel fighters."

"We?" Remi said. "You mean you. I have to go to church."

"But I need your help."

"My parents won't let me skip mass."

"But Earth needs you."

Remi shook his head. "Think about it. If I'm not at church, Father Sasseville might suspect and then tell your parents."

"He might already know," I argued. "He knew who I was."

"Duh. You're the only Chinese kid in town."

"Alien in Chinese disguise," I corrected him.

"You know what I mean. It's not hard to guess who your dad is."

I whined, "That's a lot of houses I have to check by myself."

"We have to pretend everything is normal," Remi said. You just have to find one person. Start with the new houses in town. They're the farthest away from the church. There may be people who don't want to travel that far for mass."

"Okay, but keep your eyes open during the service. Make a list of people who aren't under mind control."

"How am I supposed to figure that out?"

"I don't know. Think of something. I have to walk around town in the freezing cold."

Remi grumbled but agreed. We separated with a plan to meet up after mass.

The next morning, the church bells rang to signal the start of mass and the start of my mission. Remi told me I had about an hour before the service ended, so I had to move fast. I jogged along the snow-covered sidewalk, past the bank, the newspaper office, the video store. I caught my breath just across the street from the IGA in the centre of Bouvier, then I continued running east to the new development area.

I approached the first house, waded through a huge snowdrift in front of the porch, and rang the doorbell. No answer. I ran to the next house and rang that door. No answer there either. I ran from house to house, down one block and up another one. Was anyone at home?

I wondered if the entire town had filled the church. As I got further into the new development, the houses looked more expensive and the snow drifts seemed higher. I panted as I ploughed through the snow-covered sidewalks and stumbled to yet another empty house.

The houses lined only one side of this block. Across the street sat the Boissonault farm, which boasted the only hill in all of Bouvier. Only the French kids were allowed to ride their toboggans here. The Boissonault brothers banned all Anglais from the hill.

I tore my gaze away from the fun-looking snow hill and counted the houses along the block. There were so many that I didn't know if I could check them all before Church ended. Did Frank and Joe Hardy ever have cases as tough as this one?

I jogged to a house with a freshly-shovelled walk. A good sign. I walked up the cement steps of the house and pushed the doorbell. While I waited for someone to answer, I jogged on the spot to build up some body heat. I heard a faint noise on the other side of the door. Excited, I pressed the doorbell repeatedly.

A man's voice from inside called out. "In a minute. I'm coming. I'm coming."

I jammed my hands under my armpits. I hoped the homeowner would invite me into his warm house, so I could talk about the alien invasion over a cup of hot chocolate. I hoped the guy would believe my story. I hoped that the feeling would return to my toes. Finally, the door opened.

It was Greg, the barber's son. He looked like he had just crawled out of bed. He ran his hand through his rumpled hair. He wore a ratty pair of sweats and a T-shirt that read "Loser and proud of it." His runny nose shone bright red.

"What do you want?" he said stuffed up.

Why did it have to be Greg? Why couldn't I find a nice guy to help defeat the aliens?

"Come on, I don't have all day," he barked.

"Does anyone else live here?"

"Yeah. My mom and dad. What do you want?"

"Are they here?"

"No, they're at church."

"When was the last time you went to church?" I said.

"If you're pushing pamphlets, I'm not interested. I don't believe in religion."

This jerk could be Earth's only hope.

"I have a story to tell you," I pleaded.

"I'm not buying." Greg started to close the door. I blocked it with my boot.

"I'm not trying to sell you anything."

"Get lost, kid." He sneezed three times.

"It's about the aliens."

"The what?"

"Our planet is in real trouble. The aliens are planning an invasion."

"Oh yeah? Well, I've got Sasquatch in the basement and the Loch Ness Monster in my garage."

"You have to believe me."

Greg kicked my foot out of the doorway and slammed the door shut. I wasn't going to give up. I pressed the doorbell again.

"Just hear me out," I yelled.

I listened for his reply, but he just sneezed. Suddenly, in the distance, the church bells rang. Church service was over. I had run out of time.

The next day, I wanted to tell Remi about my failure, but I couldn't get near him. A full-scale war between the French and English students had broken out. The Boissonault brothers and their gang sought revenge for the attack on Remi.

When I walked close to Remi, Jean Boissonault spotted me. "Sneak attack," he yelled.

Jean and two other French boys hurled snowballs. I scrambled away and ran straight into Trina Brewster. We fell into a snow bank, my body on top of hers.

Trina was furious until she saw snowballs pelt the ground around us.

She whispered in my ear, "You're so brave to protect me."

I stammered, "That's not what I am — You think? No, I'm not doing that."

"Modest and brave." She beamed at me.

Trina made me feel weird. I still hated her for organizing the freak-a-zoid tour, but I also felt something else. She made my cheeks burn hot in the middle of winter. I rolled off her and ran away as fast as I could. My French attackers chased me. Trina yelled at the boys to leave me alone, but it only spurred them to run faster.

"Get her boyfriend," Jean yelled.

My cheeks burned hot again. I put my head down and sprinted hard. Suddenly, I tripped and sprawled face first into a drift. The next thing I knew, someone jumped on my back and stuck my head in the snow.

I heard Remi's voice call out, "Don't worry, I got this one. There are three over there."

"Good eye Remi," Jean called out. "Charge!"

Remi pulled my head out of the snow. "You okay?"

I spit out a mouthful of snow. "Yeah. Thanks," I said. "So what did you see at the church yesterday?"

Remi whispered, "It's not safe to talk at school any more. The war is too big."

All around us, the French and English fired snowballs and insults at one another. Remi was right.

I whispered, "Meet me behind the store after school."

"Okay," Remi said. "Sorry, I have to do this."

Remi kicked snow into my face and ran off. Two English guys ambushed him. Three French boys joined the fray. Then more soldiers from both sides charged at each other. I slunk away from the out-of-control battle.

Remi took a long time to get to the store. I asked him what kept him, but he wouldn't say a thing. Instead, he played with the face shield of his hockey helmet and avoided my eyes.

"Did you find anything at church?" I asked. I expected Remi to have better news than me.

"Tell me how you did first."

"No. You go."

"You go," Remi said.

"Did you make a list?"

"Did you find anyone to help us?" Remi seemed to be stalling.

"I asked you first."

"I asked you first," Remi echoed.

"What happened?" we said at the exact same time.

"Jinx," Remi yelled. He punched me in the arm.

"Ow."

"Double jinx." He punched me again.

"Quit it."

He punched me a third time. I bit my lip but didn't say a thing. We stood in the snow, silent for several minutes just looking at each other. Remi finally uncurled his fist.

"Why did you hit me?"

"Because we said the same thing at the same time."

"What?"

"It's a game. If we say the same thing at the same time, it's a jinx. And we get to punch each other. First one to punch wins. Double jinx happens if you say anything right after I punch you."

"You're playing games at a time like this?" My arm really hurt.

"Sorry."

"Just for that, you have to tell me what happened in the church first."

Remi looked down at his helmet. "I don't know."

"What do you mean you don't know."

Remi mumbled. "I fell asleep."

"What?!"

Remi explained, "Father Sasseville was telling a really long story. I only closed my eyes for a second. But when I looked up, people were leaving the church. I wrote down some names of people who we can trust."

"Who?"

"My mom and dad. And my sisters."

"I can't believe you fell asleep. All you had to do was one simple thing."

"It doesn't matter. You found someone who can help us, right?"

"Um. Sort of."

"What do you mean sort of?"

"Do you remember Greg from the barbershop?"

"That loud mouth? He's the king of monkey butts. Oh no. It's him. Isn't it?"

I nodded.

Remi slammed his helmet against the wall. It bounced back and hit him in the face. "Ouch!"

"Did it hurt?" I asked. As soon as I said it, I knew what Remi would say, and I tried to beat him to the punch.

"Duh," we both yelled at the same time.

"Jinx." I said. Then I smacked him in the arm.

"Ow."

"Double jinx." I punched him again. "Now we're even."

"Who's playing games now?"

"Sorry."

"So did Greg believe you?" Remi asked as he rubbed his nose.

I broke the bad news. Greg didn't believe that aliens were invading Earth. In fact, no one would believe us.

Remi slumped against the cement wall. We would receive no help against the invasion.

Suddenly, Remi smacked himself in the forehead.

"You don't have to beat yourself up over this," I said.

"No. No. Don't you get it?"

"Is this some trick like the jinx thing?"

"Who's going to believe aliens are invading Earth?"

"No one."

"Not in town, but there are believers. Who?"

It took me a minute to come up with an answer. "People who think aliens are on Earth?"

"Exactly. And who are those people?"

"You. And Me."

"And…?"

I shook my head.

"The people who wrote that U.F.O. magazine!"

Of course, the magazine people would be thrilled to learn about the alien invasion. Why hadn't I thought of that before?

Remi beamed, "Let's get that magazine of yours."

Inside my room, Remi and I barricaded the door with my dresser. We wrapped tin foil around our heads to prevent my mom from picking up our thoughts. Then we opened the U.F.O. magazine and looked for a way to contact the magazine people. We flipped past an ad for instant muscles, an ad for song-writing lessons, and a ton of classifieds selling movie star posters. Finally, I found what we needed in a tiny box on the third last page. A small ad read:

"Reward for U.F.O. evidence
Call 1-212-555-9000
New York, New York"

With one phone call, we could stop the alien invasion. We could save Earth just like that. It almost seemed too easy. Remi and I gave each other high fives.

"Where's the phone?" Remi asked.

It hit me like a ton of bricks. I groaned, "It's beside the cash register. Where Dad spends all his time."

"We could use the phone at my place," Remi suggested.

Remi was on a roll. He had two good ideas in one day.

"Then I can teach you how to play hockey," he said.

"You bet," I said.

Remi and I shoved the dresser out of the way. I threw open the door. Mom stood in the hallway, waiting for us.

"Aiya! Take off that tin foil," she barked in alienese.

I suspected Mom couldn't read our minds, which made her furious.

"This is part of our homework," I lied. "We can't take off the tin foil."

"Yes," Remi backed me up. "We have to find out how long tin foil can sit on a person's head."

Remi's streak of good ideas officially came to a grinding halt. I tried to recover. "Uh, Mom, I have to go to Remi's place to study."

She shook her head. "We have to work in store. Tell your friend to go home."

"I won't be long," I said. "I'll be right back. I promise.

Then Mom said in alienese, *"You're spending too much time with that boy."*

"He's my friend."

"You don't need that kind of friend."

"What's so wrong about him?" I asked.

Instead of answering me, she turned on Remi. "You go home now."

"Sure. You coming, Marty?"

"He stay here," she said.

"Marty?" Remi's eyes seemed to ask if my mom had used her mind control powers on me.

I think she did, because I couldn't disobey my mom. Instead, I told Remi, "I'm staying here to study."

"Oh?" he said, worried.

I struggled against her mind control and won a small point. "You're going to have to study with me here in the store,"

Mom sighed, "One hour. And then he goes home. Understand."

I nodded. Then I closed my bedroom door. I tapped my tin foil helmet, to make sure Remi kept his hat on. I put my ear against the door and listened. Mom's footsteps retreated into the distance.

Sure that she had left, I turned to Remi. "We can't let her know that we might be on to her and the alien invasion. If she figures out what we know, we'll be in real big trouble."

Remi nodded. "I bet the cows knew what the aliens were up to. And that's why they got cut up."

I shook my head. When Remi's train went off the tracks, it really went off the tracks.

"We have to get to a phone," I said.

"I could go home and make the call from there," Remi suggested.

"If you leave now, my mom might suspect something's up."

Remi agreed. "Then we have to use the phone here."

We waited until Mom started to make supper to make our move. Once we were sure of her location, Remi and I headed into the store to execute our plan. When I first proposed the idea, it sounded good. But now that I had to go through with it, I wasn't so sure. Remi slapped the back of my head and told me to get some courage. I slapped his head in retaliation.

He smiled, "That's better. Let's do it."

I headed to the cash register, where Dad read his newspaper. I coughed to get his attention. "Um, Dad. Can we talk?"

He grunted, but didn't look up from his paper.

"There's a problem in the back."

"What?"

"I think something's leaking."

"Get a mop and clean it up."

"It smells funny."

"Don't smell it."

"The leak is coming from the diapers. Should I tell Mom?"

"Where is the leak?"

"The diaper shelf," I said. "So should I get Mom?"

Dad threw his newspaper down. "No. You stay here and watch the front. I'll get it."

He bolted off. I knew he'd be worried about the bottle he had hidden behind the diapers. I also knew he would freak out when he saw the opened bottle on its side. I didn't like Dad drinking anyway, so pouring the booze out didn't bother me. The important thing was that I had bought us a few minutes.

I stuck my fingers in my mouth and tried to whistle, but only air came out. I tried again. I had seen the boys in my class whistle like this. I assumed all I had to do was stick my fingers between my lips and blow. Maybe my alien lips made a whistle so high-pitched that only other aliens or dogs could hear it. I took my fingers out of my mouth and called out to Remi.

He poked his head out from behind the meat counter. "Is the coast clear?"

"Yes. Move."

He tiptoed over with the magazine. I picked up the phone and peeked past the register. Dad kneeled at the spill. He opened a package of diapers and soaked up the mess.

"The coast is clear," I whispered to Remi. "Start dialling."

He dialled as quietly as he could. The rotary dial clacked off the numbers, thundering. Remi and I looked around to see if anyone heard. No one came running. Remi dialled the rest of the numbers. The numbers clacked off like firecrackers. He covered the phone with his shirt. I checked on Dad. He was still cleaning his spilled booze from the floor. Finally, Remi finished dialling.

He shoved the receiver at me. "You talk to them."

"Get some courage," I said, shoving the receiver back at him.

He stuck his hands behind his back and shook his head. I sighed and put the receiver to my ear.

"U.F.O. hotline," a woman answered, bored.

"I have an alien to report," I said.

"Alien invasion," Remi corrected.

"How old are you?"

"Nine."

"Look, kid. I've heard all the jokes in the book. Is your fridge running? Well, you'd better go catch it. I'm wise to it all."

"This isn't a joke," I said. "I want to report an alien."

"We only take serious reports. If you don't have a photo of a U.F.O., then you're wasting my time."

"But my parents are aliens."

"Yeah, when I was your age I thought my dad was from Mars. It turned out that he was from Jersey. You'll get over it, kid.

"Is Jersey by Saturn?"

"Don't call again," she barked and hung up.

I put the phone back on its cradle.

"She wants proof," I told Remi.

"We've got the book with the alien writing."

"Not enough. She said she wanted proof of a flying saucer. Like a photo."

"We don't have that," Remi said.

"So they won't help us?"

"No. We're on our own."

"Why couldn't you be green with big ears or antenna or something alien like? You just look normal."

This was the first time anyone ever called me normal. Usually, I heard words like "Chinaman," "Slanty Eyes," or "Chink." These words made me feel as far away from normal as possible.

Remi rapped my forehead. "Hello? Earth to alien boy. What are you thinking about?"

"Uh nothing."

"There's got to be some way we can get proof."

"Yeah, but how?"

Suddenly, Remi slapped me in the arm. "I got it."

"Ow."

"Wimp."

"Am not."

"Are too."

"Shut up." I liked arguing with Remi.

Remi pulled me away from the register and whispered. "We don't have a photo of a flying saucer. But we have the real thing."

I had no idea what he was talking about.

"The real thing," he repeated.

"Sorry. I don't get it."

Remi sighed, "How did you get here?"

"I walked."

"Stop being a monkey butt. How did your family get here?"

"I don't know."

"How did they get all the way to Earth from Saturn? Think, Marty. Think."

"I guess they must have flown in a . . . in . . . a . . . "

"Flying saucer," Remi completed my sentence.

This was our first big break. All we had to do was find where my parents parked their U.F.O.

Twelve

At first, I assumed locating the flying saucer would be easy. Dad stunk at hiding things — like his bottle of rye — and if he had a say in where to park the flying saucer, I expected to find the space craft by dinner time. However, as the day wore on, I started to lose confidence.

Remi and I paced around the parking lot beside my parents' store. He believed that the asphalt was actually the top of the space ship, but his theory hit a bump when he tripped on a pothole.

"It might be a dent from an asteroid," Remi pleaded his case.

"There's nothing but dirt in the hole," I pointed out.

"The ship has to be close in case your parents have to make a quick getaway."

"But the flying saucer is probably as big as a house."

I suggested, "Maybe it's in the church. I'll bet the steeple is the top part of the ship."

Remi shook his head, "Duh! They're called flying saucers for a reason. The space ships in the magazine looked more like dinner plates."

"Well, the church is the only place big enough to hide the U.F.O."

"Fine, fine, let's go check out the church, but I'll bet you're wrong. And we'll find out that the flying saucer was under our noses all along." Remi made a point of looking down at the parking lot pavement.

I ignored him and walked to the church. He followed me up to the locked cathedral doors. I yanked at both door handles several times, hoping that one fast pull would spring a lock. No luck. I trudged through the snow to find another entrance. About halfway around the building, I sunk into a deep snow drift.

Remi pulled me out. "If your parents need to get a quick getaway, this would be terrible place to put the U.F.O. The door's always locked except on Sundays and during weddings and funerals. They'd need Father Sasseville to let them in."

"Maybe they have their own set of keys."

"Yeah. But it'd look pretty mysterious if your parents were sneaking into the church, wouldn't it? Not very secret if you ask me."

"Maybe we have a transporter beam that can instantly send us from the store to the ship."

Remi chuckled, "Don't be stupid, Marty. If they had something like that, then why would they need a flying saucer in the first place? I think the ship has to be near the store. We just haven't looked hard enough."

"I'm not going to dig up the parking lot, Remi."

"But I know where we can get shovels."

"I think we're looking in the wrong place. The ship isn't in town."

"You're crazy. The space ship has to be close. It can't be out of town limits."

"My parents could jump in the car and drive to the space ship in minutes."

"But then the flying saucer could be anywhere."

"I think it's parked underwater in Man Made Lake," I proposed. "No one would ever look for an alien craft in Man Made Lake."

"The water's frozen."

"The ice hides the flying saucer."

"Then how would your parents get to the ship? They'd have to chop through the ice. That would take hours."

Remi had me there. "Yeah, and now that I think of it, my mom can't swim."

"So do we get to dig up the parking lot?" Remi beamed.

Then it hit me.

"No. Wait. Remi. What is the one thing that you know about the prairies?"

"It's cold."

"What else?"

"My dad says the sky goes on forever."

"Anything else?"

"Oh yeah. My uncle Louis says the prairies are flatter than my mom's pancakes."

"Exactly. It's all flat. Except for where?"

Remi scrunched his face like he had just sucked on a lemon. I think that was his thinking look.

His eyes popped wide open. "The snow hill in the Boissonault's field!"

"Exactly."

"The flying saucer is under the hill."

We had just cracked the case of the missing U.F.O.

Remi pointed out, "Mr. Boissonault hates it when we go sledding on his field. He says he gets too many calls from Moms wanting their kids to go home. Now he doesn't let anyone on the hill."

"But we have to get to the flying saucer. It's the only way we can prove there's an alien invasion."

"It's not going to be easy," he said. "He's a mean old man."

I disagreed with Remi. Mr. Boissonault was nice to our family, even though his sons, Jean and Jacques, were jerks to me. He was one of the few people who still shopped at my parents' store after the IGA opened. During hunting season, he always brought in a deer for my dad to butcher. And every Christmas, Mr. Boissonault sent us a nice card.

However, when new houses popped up all around his farm land, he became grumpy to everyone. I think he hated how fast the town grew, and he fenced off his land to make sure the town didn't spill over onto his land. Mr. Boissonault had put up "No Trespassing" signs all along his barbed-wire fence. He didn't want anyone setting foot on his property.

Remi and I walked on the other side of his fence toward the big hill. We had to be very careful if we were going to sneak on to the Boissonault field, because the hill stood in plain sight of the farmhouse.

Remi guessed the distance from the fence to the hill to be fifty feet. I estimated the time to run that far would be at least a minute. We glanced back at the farmhouse and the black truck parked in front. Smoke billowed out of the chimney. The lights in the living room burned bright. Someone was definitely home. If we squinted, we probably could see Mr. Boissonault sitting in his easy chair on the lookout for trespassers.

I looked at the long stretch between the fence and the hill and sighed, "We'll never make it without him seeing us. Maybe if we waited until it got a little darker. Then it'd be harder to see us."

Suddenly, Remi dropped on his belly and pulled me down with him.

"I have a better idea," he said. "Crawl."

Remi slithered through the snow using his elbows as snow ploughs. When he reached the barbed wire fence, he lowered his head and squirmed under. I crawled behind him, but he moved too fast for me to keep up.

"Stay down until we get behind the hill," Remi shouted back. "Try not to breathe or they'll see the puffs."

I held my breath and inched through the cold snow. I heard a door slam in the distance. I glanced at the farmhouse. The coast was clear. I continued to crawl through the snow.

When I reached the back side of the hill, Remi was already digging snow away from the slope. I joined him. While we could easily clear the snow away, the frozen dirt posed a bigger problem. Our mittens barely made a dent in the hard black surface.

"This is going to take forever," I told Remi.

He agreed, "Yeah, it sucks if you want to make a fast getaway."

"If I hid the space ship here, I'd make a fake section of the hill where the door is. It'd look like part of the hill, but one tug of a branch and the flying saucer door would swing open. I wouldn't have to dig at all."

"Yeah, it would make sense. Do you think your dad did that?"

"Maybe. We just have to find the fake part of the hill."

"I knew I should have brought my dad's shovels."

I noticed some branches had fallen from the birch saplings at the top of the hill. I picked up two and handed one to Remi.

"What am I supposed to do with this?" he asked.

I stabbed the hill with my branch. It made a dull thud in the frozen dirt.

"When you hear the branch hit something metal, then we've found the door."

"You aliens are pretty smart," Remi said.

He jabbed the hill with his stick. Together, we poked the entire side of the hill. My face became numb from the chilly wind. Remi's face almost glowed red. I leaned against a tree and caught my breath, while Remi clapped his hands to warm them. We had not found the door.

"It's got to be here," I said.

"I'll bet the door's at the top of the hill."

I agreed. We started to climb. Halfway up, we heard a faint noise. We stopped and listened.

Crunch, crunch, crunch.

Footsteps, coming around the hill toward us.

"Run!" Remi said as he scrambled down the hill.

As I followed him down the hill, my boot wedged under a tree root and refused to budge.

"Remi," I called. "I'm stuck."

He skidded to a stop and returned to help me. He knelt down and lifted the root up. I pulled my foot out.

"Well, well," said a voice behind us.

We turned to face Jacques Boissonault. Just behind him, Jean carried a rifle.

"What do we have here?" Jacques continued.

"Trespassers," said Jean as he hid the rifle behind his back.

"What are we going to do with them?"

Remi explained, "We were taking a short cut."

I nodded, too scared to say anything.

"Cat got your tongue?" asked Jacques.

"Their kind don't talk much," said his brother.

"He talks just fine," Remi defended me.

I squeaked, "Yes. I can talk."

"Shut up!" Jacques barked.

He advanced on us, while Jean hung back.

"We should teach these trespassers a lesson," threatened Jacques.

His brother agreed. "Got some yellow snow they could eat?"

"The Chinaman probably likes eating yellow things."

Jean let loose a high-pitched laugh.

Despite the cold, I could feel my face burn red hot. I wanted so badly to find the flying saucer so that I could return to Saturn.

Remi came to my rescue, "Stop calling him that. He's my friend."

"And after we took on the Anglais for you," Jacques said. "You're a traitor."

"He's better than you," I defended Remi.

"Shut your mouth China—" Jean corrected himself. "I mean chink."

"Take that back," Remi said.

"You gonna to make us?" Jacques advanced on us.

"You take another step and you'll be sorry," Remi warned.

The Boissonaults didn't stop. Instead, Remi backed up. He grabbed the back of my jacket and pulled me with him.

"Get ready to run," he whispered.

I didn't know what Remi had in mind, but anything was better than these two lug heads pounding on us.

Jean taunted us, "You gonna show us some kung fu, petite Chinois?"

Jacques laughed. "Yeah, let's seem him break some boards with his yellow face."

"You won't be laughing so hard when we get through with you," Remi said.

"The two of you against us?" Jacques laughed.

"No, all of the Anglais are on top of the hill," Remi smiled at me.

I picked up on Remi's hint. I added, "Yeah, this is one big trap."

"Bull," Jacques spat out.

Jean seemed less sure than his brother. "What if he's telling the truth, Jacques?"

"He's bluffing, Jean."

Remi stuck his fingers in his mouth and whistled sharply.

"Okay, boys! Let them have it," he yelled.

Jean and Jacques stepped back and looked up for snowball snipers. For a second, neither of them moved.

Remi shoved me.

"Run!" he yelled.

We bolted for the barbed-wire fence, wading through the deep snow. The Boissonaults sprang into action and chased us. Heavier than us, they sunk deeper into the snow drifts. Remi ploughed through the snow like a mad bull, while I followed in his tracks. Behind us, the Boissonaults started to gain ground.

"Remi! We can't make it," I yelled.

"Keep going," he shouted, not even looking back.

Jean and Jacques screamed all sorts of threats. They vowed to make us roll around in cow poop. They swore they would rip off our clothes and send us home naked. They promised to hang us up in the barn and use us as punching bags. Each threat spurred me to run even faster. I pushed Remi forward, desperate to escape the Boissonault nightmare.

"We've got trouble," Remi yelled.

He pointed at the section of the barbed-wire fence, which offered no space for us to squeeze under. Meanwhile, the brothers gained ground.

"They're coming," I screamed. "They're going to turn us into poop-sicles."

Remi charged the barbed wire. He reached out and grabbed the top wire and put his head down.

He yelled, "Climb on my back and go over the fence."

"What about you?"

"Just climb over me!"

I scrambled up his back and threw myself over the fence. I flipped in mid-air and sunk butt first into the snow drift. I scrambled to my feet and turned to help my friend.

Remi shouted, "Grab the top wire and hold it up."

I grabbed the wire and stretched it as high as I could. One of the barbs pierced through my mitten and bit into my hand, but I wasn't going to let go until Remi was safe. As Remi stepped through, his parka caught on one of the barbs. Remi struggled to get free. He screamed as the barb dug into his shoulder.

Jacques closed the gap. Jean had trouble running with the rifle strapped across his back. But the brothers could walk and easily catch the trapped Remi.

I strained to lift the wire higher. More of Remi's jacket ripped. Then I saw the problem and the solution.

"Remi, back up and then duck!" I yelled.

He hesitated for a second, but then followed my instructions. His parka popped free.

"Now come through," I shouted.

Remi dove through the gap between the wires just as Jacques reached the fence. I pulled Remi out of Jacques's long reach and we stumbled into the ditch, safe from the angry Boissonault. Jacques howled at us. Then he tried to squirm under the barbed wire. He was too big to get through. He grabbed Jean and tried to toss him over the fence, but Jean fought his brother off.

Remi and I ran down the road toward town. Jacques threatened to get even with us. Jean yelled out that they'd find us at school. Remi and I ran until their yells were faint in the distance.

I could barely breathe, but Remi sprinted effortlessly. His hockey conditioning gave him a lot of stamina; however, my chest felt like it was going to burst open. I slowed down and flagged Remi to stop for a second.

"I think we're safe now," I panted. "Besides, I wanted to take a look at your jacket."

Remi waved me off.

"No big deal. The Anglais already ripped it once. I'll get Mom to sew it up again. How are you doing?"

I took off my mittens. My right palm had a little blood from the barbed-wire, but the cold had numbed the pain. I wiped my palm. It stung a little, but there was no more blood.

"That was wild. I'd never done that before," I said.

"I don't want to do it again."

"But we have to get to the flying saucer."

"Not with the brothers guarding it." Remi glanced back nervously.

"They're not guarding the flying saucer," I argued. "They don't even know it's there. It was just dumb luck that we ran into them."

"I don't think it was a coincidence," Remi argued. "I think they're working for the aliens."

"What? How can you be so sure?"

"They're Father Sasseville's altar boys."

I was stunned. "You mean they work for the Night Watchman?"

"They're his favourites."

"Oh boy, this is starting to make sense," I said. "It's not enough to just hide the flying saucer. My parents also have to protect it. And the Boissonaults make perfect guards."

"They must be using mind control on them."

"Wait a minute," I said. "Why do they hate me if they're under alien control?"

Remi said, "I don't know. Maybe your parents can't control what humans think, just what they do. Or maybe Jean and Jacques are jealous that you come from another planet."

I never considered that anyone would want to be like me, especially the Boissonaults.

Remi said, "Now that the brothers know we tried to get into the flying saucer, they're going to be watching it real close. We'll never get past them."

He sighed as he pulled at the loose stuffing from his jacket. As I watched him pick at the fluffy white material, an idea formed.

"Remi. You know how you got free from the fence?"

He nodded.

"This is the same thing," I said. "Maybe we're trying too hard to go forward."

"So we should go backwards?"

"Not backwards. But sideways. If we can't beat the brothers, maybe we can bribe them."

"I've got like two dollars and some change. I don't think that's enough."

"Not money. Ice cream."

"Huh," Remi almost went cross-eyed trying to figure out the logic of my plan.

"Their dad buys ice cream at my parents' store. He says Jean goes nuts for strawberry. I figure if there's enough strawberry ice cream, Jean might look the other way."

"What about Jacques?"

"I think he likes chocolate."

"Let's get Neapolitan. Less pails to carry."

I smiled. "I like the way you think."

Sneaking Remi into the store got harder every time. My mom tensed up whenever she saw him. I believed that she suspected we were on to her invasion plans. I figured the less Mom saw of Remi, the better. This would give us the element of surprise.

Remi waited for me in the alley, while I ran into the store. I waved at Dad as I jogged past him.

"You're late," he growled.

"Sorry," I mumbled. I turned around.

"You were playing with your friend again," he accused.

"No." I sort of told the truth. Remi and I were not playing. We were trying to save the world.

"Where is he now?"

"He went home I think."

"You finish your homework?" Dad barked. Ever since his bottle of rye spilled on the floor, Dad was pretty cranky.

"I did all my homework at school," I said.

"Then do your chores," He snapped. "There is a lot of work to do."

"Where's Mom?" I asked.

"She's cooking. You tell her I'm not hungry." When Dad made me pass messages to Mom, it meant they were fighting.

"Okay," I said.

"Don't be late any more," Dad growled.

At the back of the store, Remi and I crept to the ice cream freezer, which was located near the kitchen. Behind the closed door, Mom clattered pots and pans loudly. This was her way of letting off steam.

As long as my parents fought with each other, they wouldn't worry about some missing ice cream. I dug my fingers under the freezer lid and heaved it up. The pressure of the vacuum seal held the lid shut. I kept pushing until . . . thwock . . . the rubber seal broke free and the lid popped open. Cold air blasted my face.

Remi looked inside and nearly drooled on the ice cream. "It's my dream come true," he whispered.

"Hold the lid open," I said.

"You got chocolate-covered bars! I love them."

I shushed Remi, but he wouldn't listen.

"And soft sundae ice cream with the wooden spoons. You are so lucky."

"Shh, my mom's gonna hear you."

"I'm lucky if my parents' freezer has a Nutty Buddy. Oh wow, there's a box of them!"

"Just hold the lid, Remi."

He reluctantly took over. As he held up the lid, he ogled the pails of ice cream. I leaned into the freezer, moved the ice cream aside in search of the distinctive Neapolitan swirl. Goosebumps popped up along my cold arms. My fingers went numb. My glasses fogged up.

"Hey, what's that?" Remi whispered.

He pointed to the corner of the freezer to three frozen plastic bags. I wiped my lenses and grabbed one of the bags. It was about the size of a head of lettuce, but it was heavier than lettuce. I brushed the frost off the plastic covering.

"What kind of ice cream is that?" he asked.

"I don't think it's ice cream," I said. "Give me a minute."

I rubbed the frost off, then held the bag up to Remi's face. He let out a short yelp and backed away. I turned the bag around and looked inside.

"Yikes!" I dropped the bag on the floor.

The hideous thing inside the bag looked like someone had mushed a giant batch of grey Play-Doh into a weird ball.

"Is that . . . is that . . . I think it is . . . no way . . . it looks like . . . no way . . . "

"It looks like a brain," I said.

Remi shuddered and looked away from the brain bag on the tiled floor. We had found three bags of brains in my parents' ice cream freezer. The big question was whose brains?

THIRTEEN

The next day, I could barely concentrate on Mrs. Connor's lesson. All I could think about were the brains in the freezer. What did my parents want to do with them? Were the brains some part of the invasion plan? What happened to the people with the missing brains? Were they still alive? Who were they?

Mrs. Connor pulled me out of my thoughts and pushed me into her lesson. "Mr. Chan, were you paying attention?"

"Uh. Yes, Mrs. Connor," I lied.

"Then would you care to repeat to the class exactly I just said?"

I scanned the white board for some kind of clue. Mrs. Connor had written the word "Prejudice" in red. I knew what the colour meant. She wanted us to define the word. Red was for definitions. Blue was for homework assignments. Black was for pop quiz questions.

I launched into the definition, "Prejudice is the act of making assumptions about people based on how they look or what they do. 'Pre' means before and 'judice' is like judging. You should get to know people before you think the worst of them."

"Very good," Mrs. Connor cooed. "That's exactly what we should do. But it's not what I just said. I asked if anyone had seen Ms. Brewster or Mr. Johnson."

My classmates laughed at me. I looked around. The two desks where Trina Brewster and Eric Johnson normally sat were empty.

"What's so funny?" Mrs. Connor asked, using her patented question technique to get everyone to shut up.

Trina's empty desk sparked big questions. What could have happened to her and Eric? Had the attack started? Why did I miss the girl who bugged me so much? I raised my hand.

"Yes Mr. Chan?" Ms. Connor said.

"Do you think something bad happened to Trina?"

The other kids snickered.

"No, Mr. Chan."

"Maybe we should check on her."

Some of my classmates giggled. One guy whispered to the others that Trina was my girlfriend.

"I'm worried about Eric too," I quickly added.

"Well, I'm sure they'll be fine. Now let's get back to the lesson." Mrs. Connor turned to the white board and took out her black pen. Pop quiz. Everyone groaned.

Mrs. Connor wrote math problems on the white board, but I barely noticed them. Instead, I computed a different set of math calculations in my head. Three brains in the freezer. Two missing students. Who was the third?

At lunch, I searched the schoolyard for Remi. I didn't care if anyone saw us together. The invasion had started. Eventually, I found him sitting by himself under the Jesus statue. The other French boys ran around in the field, playing with each other and ignoring him.

"Why aren't you out there?" I asked.

"The Boissonaults told everyone about me and you. Now no one will talk to me."

"Sorry."

"I don't have any friends now."

"You've got me."

Remi didn't say a thing. My stomach twisted in a big knot. I wondered what would have happened if I had never told Remi my secret. Would he still have friends?

"You don't need them," I said. "They're not real friends if they force you to pick who hang with."

"I play hockey with most of them. They're gonna cream me at the next practice."

"That's not important."

"I'm going to be the meat in a body check sandwich."

"What?"

"Duh, monkey butt." He held up one hand and slammed his fist into it. "Get the picture?"

I nodded. "But there won't be a hockey practice. The aliens have started their invasion."

"What?" Remi stood up, worried.

I told him about Trina's and Erics' mysterious disappearance from class, but I pointed out that there were three brains in the freezer.

Remi punched his hand. "The invasion has started. Norman Arsenault didn't show up for class today. Mrs. Riopel said he was at home sick, but Norman's got the record for perfect attendance. He'd have to be really sick to miss class."

"The aliens have them," I suggested.

"What do the aliens want to do with three kids?"

"Brace yourself. I have a theory."

"Does it have anything to do with cows?" Remi asked.

"No. In a couple of days, Norman, Eric and Trina will show up at school. But they'll be different."

"Different like how?"

"They'll have alien brains."

"Brain-napping! Are you serious, Marty?"

"Yes. Three frozen brains and three missing students. It all adds up."

"But the aliens can't be here yet. We haven't seen any U.F.O.s in the sky."

"Jean and Jacques probably told Father Sasseville about us snooping around the hill. Maybe the aliens decided to speed up the take over. I think they're getting humans ready for some kind of brain transfer."

Remi said, "But what are they doing with Norman, Eric and Trina until the aliens get here?"

I imagined the trio strapped into metal chairs on the flying saucer. Their heads were popped open and their skulls empty. When I thought about Trina, my heart pumped out a lump that shot straight to my throat. My legs went weak.

"Remi, we have to sneak into the flying saucer now. The Boissonaults are at school. No one's guarding the flying saucer. We have to save Trina! And Eric and Norman too."

"Let's rock and roll," Remi shouted.

We headed out of the schoolyard, but the Boissonaults intercepted us.

Jean screamed, "Remi's with the Chinaman again. Get them."

About twenty French boys chased us, with Jacques screaming for more people to help catch us.

"I think the Boissonaults are on to us," I yelled to Remi. "They're not going to let us out of their sight."

"Get the chinaman," yelled Jacques.

"Ignore him," Remi yelled. "Just keep running."

We were too far from the school building to get help from the teachers, and there were too many guys after us. I started to run out of steam as the French boys gained ground.

"Marty," Remi panted. He pointed at a group of Anglais building a snow fort. He remembered how I got rid of the students on Trina's freak-a-zoid tour.

I smiled.

We sprinted toward the snow fort. Behind us, the French kids continued to charge.

"Get them!" Jacques ordered his army.

"Attack the French," I yelled at the group of Anglais.

The English kids scrambled out of the fort and ran toward us. The air filled with war whoops and threats.

Suddenly, both sides stopped dead in their tracks. The reason why was Principal Henday. He stepped between the two warring parties. He looked from one group to the other.

"I'm disappointed in all of you," he clucked. "I've had enough of this fighting in the schoolyard. You are all to spend recesses and lunch hours in your classes washing the windows and cleaning the gum off the bottom of the desks."

Everyone moaned.

"Half of the French will work in the English classes, and half of the English boys will be in the French classes. That's the only way you are going to learn to get along."

No one looked happy about this truce. I could hear people mutter about "The Rake's" unfair punishment. The French guys agreed with the Anglais.

Mr. Henday silenced everyone. "Or I could just call all your parents and tell them what you were doing. Would you like that?"

Everyone shut up. I wondered if Mrs. Connor had taught Mr. Henday how to get people to shut up.

Mr. Henday barked, "Your punishment starts now. Everybody inside."

Everyone filed toward the school. Remi and I took our time and let the pack get ahead of us.

I whispered to Remi, "What do we do now?"

He shrugged. "We're stuck at school. And I'm sure the Boissonaults will rush home to protect the hill. There's no way we can get into the spaceship."

"Maybe my Dad has a ray gun or something. We can use it to shrink the Boissonaults and get past them." I liked the thought of a two-inch high Jacques Boissonault.

Remi agreed. "We'll search the store for a weapon, then we can storm the hill."

After school, I headed into the store to let Remi in through the back. But when I walked past the cash register, I had to stop. My dad was talking with the Night Watchman.

"Everything is almost ready, George," said Father Sasseville.

"Do you think there will be any problems?" asked Dad.

"Maybe some red tape, but nothing I can't take care of."

Red tape? Was this some kind of special code for Remi and me? Father Sasseville looked right at me.

"Good to see you again, my son," he said.

"Uh . . . hi."

"Have you given any more thought to your conversion?"

"What?" Dad asked.

"I'm still thinking about it. I have to get to work. Excuse me."

I shuffled up the aisle. Dad turned back to Father Sasseville. "So when will they get here?"

"If all works out, very soon."

"I can pick them up," Dad offered.

"That would be good. I'll let you know when everything is ready. We have to move quickly, so be ready."

I didn't need to hear any more. I rushed to the back of the store. I let Remi in and told him about Father Sasseville's conversation with my dad.

"They're speeding up the invasion," I said. "We have to rescue the brains."

We headed to the freezer. Remi unzipped his backpack, while I lifted the freezer lid. We looked at the bags of brains nestled in the corner beside the ice cream pails. Each bag seemed to pulse with its individual brain. I would never eat ice cream again without thinking about Trina's frozen brain in the freezer.

"Okay, you grab the bags. I'll hold the backpack open," Remi said.

"What? No, you get them. I'll hold the lid up."

"We don't have time to argue. Get the brains." Remi held open his pack.

"I'm not touching them."

"Are you scared?"

"No. Are you?"

"Just put the brains in my backpack, Marty."

"Rock, paper, scissors decides." I held up my hand.

Remi sighed and held out his hand. We counted off. One. Two. Three. He had rock. I had paper. Remi grumbled and shoved his pack at me, then leaned into the freezer and gingerly picked up the bags by their twist ties.

The first bag dropped into the pack like a stone. The next one thudded hard against the first brain.

"Careful. That could have been Trina's brain," I said.

"You like her or something?"

"No," I lied. "Just be careful."

"Sure, sure. I'll be careful with your girlfriend's brain."

He picked up the third brain bag and juggled it around.

"Careful," I said.

"Ooops," Remi joked as he tossed the bag from one hand to another. "I just about dropped your girlfriend's brain."

"Don't."

"Whoa, she's got a slippery brain."

"Careful!"

"Ooops, just about dropped it again."

"You jerk!"

"Aiya!" My mom's voice stopped Remi in mid toss. The bagged brain clattered on the tiled floor and slid to her feet.

Wearing a bloody apron, Mom picked up the tiny brain bag. I figured by the size it had to be Eric Johnson's noggin. I hoped it wasn't Trina's.

Mom yelled in alienese, *"What are you doing?"*

"Nothing," I mumbled.

She held up the brain bag and barked. "Put them back."

Remi and I didn't budge, petrified of my mom.

"Now!" she screamed.

Her angry glare triggered her mind control powers. Instead of arguing with her, we obeyed without question. Remi took the brain from Mom's hand, while I snatched the two brains in my backpack and laid them back into the freezer. Remi handed me the third brain and I placed it on top of the other two. We closed the freezer and turned to face my mom.

"Tell your friend to go home now."

"I can explain Mom."

"Now!" She used the mind control glare again.

"I should get going anyway," Remi said. He grabbed the backpack from me. "I'll see you tomorrow at school."

I wanted to tell him to get help, but my mouth dried up and my lips couldn't make a sound. Instead, I just watched my friend leave me alone with a very mad alien mom. I tried to apologize to her, but she used her mind control glare to shut me up.

"You will never see that boy again."

I struggled against her mind control and protested, "But he's my friend."

"I don't care."

"He's my only friend."

"A real friend would not make so much trouble for you. Go to your room," she barked.

I obeyed. As I walked down the hall, I could feel her cold glare pierce through the back of my head and force me to shamble to my room.

I reviewed what had gone wrong. Mom must have read our minds. If we had worn our tin foil helmets, we would never have been caught, and Earth might be saved. And Trina's brain wouldn't be sitting on top of a box of Freezies.

In my bedroom, I listened to the cement wall for Remi's secret knock. I watched the clock count off the minutes, then an hour. No knock came. Remi had gone home. Mom's mind control glare must have been pretty powerful.

In bed, I focussed on the problem at hand. The aliens were on their way. Father Sasseville and the Boissonaults probably doubled security around the flying saucer. And now that Mom knew I was on to her, she would be doubling security around me.

I got up and paced around my room. There had to be some way to thwart the invasion or at least give the humans a fighting chance. I saw Remi running from a giant flying saucer. I saw Father Sasseville ordering the Boissonault brothers to round up all the kids at school. I saw the freezer fill up with human brains. I saw myself taking out Trina's brain and putting it back into her pretty head. I saw myself eating lunch with her and holding her hand. I shook off the daydream. How could I have such mixed feelings about this girl?

Before I could come up with an answer, I stubbed my toe on something hard. I muffled a yelp and hopped around the room. When my toe stopped throbbing, I looked under my bed and found Remi's hockey helmet, which he had left behind. I examined the chin strap and the face shield. This thing was sturdy. If a human wore it, his brain would be protected from anything, even aliens.

I had to find more helmets.

FOURTEEN

I wasn't the only one looking for Remi the next morning. Jean and Jacques had organized a search party. The Boissonault brothers and their posse scoured the schoolyard. I hid behind the Jesus statue and overheard two French guys talk about how they wanted to get revenge on Remi for getting everyone in trouble. They also mentioned me. I snuck away.

Half-way across the schoolyard, someone yelled, "There he is!"

It was James Crane from my home room. He waved the French kids over and they chased after me. Other Anglais students followed. "The Rake's" plan had worked. For the first time ever, the French and the English were side by side. The only problem was that they were working together to get me.

The school bell rang to start class. I sprinted into the building where I would be safe under the watchful eyes of Mrs. Connor and Principal Henday. I looked around the boot room for Remi, but I didn't see him.

I figured he was laying low just as I should have been. I figured I would find him later.

At recess, however, Remi did not show up for cleaning detail in my classroom, which left me alone against some of the meanest guys in school. Both the French and English boys snapped their cleaning towels at my butt. I rushed to a corner of the class and jammed my bum against the wall. The boys made up reasons to "clean" the corner and snapped towels at my legs. I blocked their towels with my arms, which soon burned bright red.

Mrs. Connor cut off the attack when she strolled in to check on the noise in class. The boys went back to work, while I nursed my sore arms. I wondered if Remi was suffering the same fate in his classroom. I planned to check on him at lunch hour.

But he was not in his classroom at noon. Instead, I ran into the Boissonaults. Jacques smacked a wet mop between my legs so that it looked like I had peed my pants. Jean laughed and offered to clean it up with his spray bottle of window cleaner. The other boys laughed. I covered myself and backed out of the classroom.

I searched the rest of the school, but Remi had vanished from the face of the Earth. Had he found a great hiding place? Or had the French/English alliance stuffed him into a locker? Either way, he was missing in action.

In one room, a crusty teacher with white hair marked homework assignments. Maybe she had seen Remi.

"Excuse me?" I squeaked.

She looked up from her papers. "About time you boys got to my class. Start with the big desk at the back. It's gum central. You'll have to scrape hard."

"Actually, I'm looking for Remi."

The crusty teacher stopped. "He didn't show up for school today. There's a flu going around. I think he might have caught it."

It seemed too convenient for Remi to be absent the very day after my mom caught us with the frozen brains.

"Did his parents tell you that?" I asked.

The teacher just shrugged. "Some woman called the school. I assume it was his mother."

Or it was my mom posing as Remi's parent. "Thanks," I mumbled to the teacher.

I shambled down the hall, stunned. Without Remi by my side, I started to lose my nerve. I found it easier to fight aliens when there were two of us. I felt like I could do anything, mainly because Remi thought he could do anything. He was so unlike my parents and teachers who mostly told me what I could not do. Now he had been brain-napped and I had no idea what to do. I couldn't possibly win this war by myself.

So lost in my thoughts, I didn't see the French and English boys sneak up on me until it was too late. I howled when the first rag snapped against my leg. They charged after me, calling out to get the Chinaman.

More English and French boys spilled out into the hallway to chase after me. I scrambled around a corner and down a hall. They kept chasing me. Where were the teachers? It hit me. They were in the only place I had not looked for Remi.

I sprinted down the hall to the teachers' lounge. I grabbed the doorknob. The mob hesitated.

One of the Anglais said, "Chill. He's going to get a teacher."

Jacques scoffed at me, "You don't have the guts."

Jean yelled, "Get him before he opens the door."

They charged at me. I froze. No student was allowed to walk into the teachers' lounge. But if I didn't go inside right now, the cleaning detail would "clean" me into the hospital. I yanked open the door and ran into the forbidden room.

I expected the teachers' lounge to look like a classroom. Instead of students' desks, I thought it would be full of teachers' desks and teachers' textbooks. I expected the teachers would be practicing how to write in big letters on white boards, or Mrs. Connor would be testing her shut-up questions on other teachers.

What I saw was nothing like I had imagined. The room had two ratty couches, a couple of chipped coffee tables, and a coffee pot. The room had no books, just a lot of scattered newspapers. The teachers weren't doing anything that looked like teaching. They just sat on the couches and ate their lunches while they stared blankly at the television which played the noon hour news. They were like zombies. No one even turned around when I came in.

Before anyone noticed me, I crept to the coffee counter. Under the coffee pot, a cupboard looked big enough to fit me. Perfect. All I had to do was hide in the cramped space long enough for the teachers to leave and for the "cleaning" posse to return to class.

I opened the cupboard door. It squeaked. I froze. None of the zombie teachers even looked over. I peeked inside the cupboard. Some sugar packets crowded a large bowl. Other than that, the shelf sat bare. I crawled into the cupboard. It was a tight fit, but I squeezed inside. A sugar packet slid under my butt, but I ignored it. I grabbed the edge of the squeaky cupboard door and pulled it closed.

The cupboard smelled of coffee and my sweat. Was there enough air in the cupboard? I sucked wind through my mouth because I couldn't stand the smell that wafted up my nose.

To pass the time, I recounted the Hardy Boy books that I had read. I tried to remember if they had any cases like mine. But as I sifted through the stories, I found that their adventures weren't as thrilling as my real-life case. I wondered if a writer would ever write about my exploits. I imagined I was the third Hardy brother: Marty Hardy. If I were the writer, I'd come up with a better name than that. I hated my name because people liked to find rhymes to go with it. The girls enjoyed "Smarty Marty." The boys really liked "Farty Marty." I wanted people to call me "Party Marty," but to earn that title, I'd have to throw a party first, and there was no way my mom would let anyone come over to our home.

Finally, the school bell rang for the start of afternoon classes. Someone turned off the television. Then the teachers grumbled about having to go back to class. It was strange to hear that even teachers didn't like to go to class.

Their footsteps headed out of the lounge. But then one set of footsteps came toward my hiding place. I tensed my butt cheeks. I hugged myself and tried to shrink to the size of a fly. All I got was a headache. The footsteps stopped right beside the cupboard. I held my breath and listened.

Glug. Glug. Glug.

The sound of coffee being poured into a cup.

Some teacher was fuelling up for the rest of the day. I unclenched my butt.

"We're out of sugar," a man's voice said.

"I think there's some around here," Mrs. Connor said.

Yes there was. Right under me. The cupboard creaked open and light punched through. I had to act fast. I reached under my bum and flicked the sugar packet out of the cupboard.

"Oh look," Mrs. Connor said. There's some here on the floor."

The door squeaked shut and darkness wrapped around me. I heard the tinkle of a spoon against a porcelain cup. The teachers were stirring their coffees. Just a few more minutes and I would be safe. Finally, the footsteps left the room. I waited a few minutes to be sure that I was alone. I would be late for class, but I'd get in less trouble for being late than being caught in the teachers' lounge.

I pushed the door open and tried to squirm out, but I couldn't move my legs. I was wedged in the cupboard.

I rocked back and forth but I didn't budge an inch. No matter how hard I tried, I could not get free. The more I struggled, the more stuck I got. I felt like Remi snagged on the barbed-wire fence, only this time I couldn't go forward or backwards. And there was no one to help me.

I took a deep breath. There had to be a way out. I just hadn't thought of it yet. I curled up into a smaller ball and tried to roll out. When I tucked my head between my legs, I let out a gross fart. Now I was stuck and stinky.

"Help," I gasped. "I'm here! Anyone! Anyone but an alien sympathizer! Help me!"

I felt like I yelled for ten minutes straight. At first, I bellowed. But as my throat got hoarser, my cries turned into whimpers. I stopped to catch my breath. And that's when I heard the lounge door open.

Re-energized, I yelled, "Help me! I'm stuck in the cupboard."

I saw a pair of legs walk closer. My saviour bent over so I could see his face. It was Jean Boissonault. Could things get any worse?

FIFTEEN

"Hey, Jacques," Jean called out. "Check this out."

Jacques Boissonault bent down and cracked a big smile. "Good thing Mrs. Riopel sent both of us to check on the noise."

"Yeah, I'd hate for you to have all the fun," Jean said. Then he looked at me. "We've been looking for you."

Jacques growled, "You and that traitor, Remi."

"Let me out," I said, feeling cramps in my neck, back, and legs.

"What's the magic word?" Jacques taunted.

"Please," I said.

"In French," Jean said.

I tried to say "please" with a French accent. It sounded more like "police."

"Stupid Chinaman," Jacques growled. "Are you making fun of the way we talk?"

Jean piped up, "He's just like the rest of them. Thinks he's too smart for us."

Jacques laughed, "He can't be that smart. Look at where he is."

Jean examined my tight quarters. "So how did you get stuck in here?"

"None of your business."

"It is if we have to pull you out," Jean said.

"Who said we were going to do that?" Jacques argued. "We still owe him for getting us in trouble with 'The Rake.'"

Jean nodded. "Yeah, let's get him out and 'thank' him for that."

"I don't need your help," I lied.

Jacques chuckled. "I think you do."

"All you're going to do is pull me out, beat me up and stick me back in the cupboard."

Jean nodded, "That's a pretty good idea. Why didn't you think of that Jacques?"

"Who said I didn't?"

"I'll tell on you," I warned.

Jacques knelt down and blasted me with his peanut butter breath. "Why did your slant-eyed parents come here in the first place, stupid chink?"

"Get out of there," Jean ordered.

"No way. I know what you're going to do to me."

Jacques threatened, "You'll get it either way."

"What do you plan to do with me? The same thing you did to Remi?"

"That yapper is going to get his soon enough," Jacques said.

The way Jacques uttered his threat made me think he knew where Remi was. I guessed the brothers held him hostage on the flying saucer inside the hill. I could almost see him strapped in a hard metal chair surrounded by the brainless Eric and Norman. I pictured Trina, helpless and brainless in another metal chair. I had to hurry if I was going to save all of them.

"I know what you did," I lied, hoping to trick the brothers into telling me what I needed.

"What did we do?" the brothers said at the exact same time.

"Jinx!" They punched each other in the arm.

"Ow! Double jinx!" More punching followed.

They glared at each other, waiting for the other one to speak again, their fists cocked and ready. It was a Boissonault stand-off.

I broke the silence, "I saw everything at the hill."

"You didn't see anything," Jacques said.

"You did a lousy job of hiding it," I continued.

"I told you it was a bad idea," Jean told his brother.

"Shut up!"

"I know everything," I bluffed.

Jean whispered, "He knows about the—"

"I said shut up." Jacques hit his brother hard in the stomach then pointed the same fist in my face. "You won't talk if you know what's good for you."

Jacques was a tough cookie, but Jean seemed ready to crumble.

I ignored Jacques' fist and called out to Jean. "You know what I'm talking about, don't you?"

"Don't listen to the Chinaman, Jean."

"Is Jacques the boss of you?"

"Shut up, chink."

Jean told his brother to leave me alone, but Jacques refused.

"You tell anyone about what you saw at the hill, you're gonna be really sorry." Jacques sounded more nervous than threatening.

"Maybe I'll tell the Father."

"Leave him out of this," Jean said.

Jacques agreed. "Our father doesn't have to know anything about this.

The Night Watchman scared even Jacques Boissonault. I had some leverage. If I kept pushing, the brothers would tell me how to get into the spaceship.

"Maybe we can work something out," I said.

"Forget it," Jacques spat. "I don't make deals with Chinamen."

"Let's listen to him," Jean said.

"No, let's punch him until he promises to keep his mouth shut."

"I'll talk no matter what you do," I said.

Jacques pulled his brother away. "Jean, no one's going to believe that stupid kid."

"If Father finds out we snuck out with his rifle, we're dead."

Why were they talking about a rifle? I remembered seeing them with a gun at the hill, but I assumed they used it to guard the spaceship. As I re-played the snow hill escape in my mind, I remembered that Jean had tried very hard to hide the rifle. He didn't want Remi and me to know he had it.

I called out, "You tell me where Remi is and maybe I'll think about keeping quiet about the gun."

Jacques and Jean looked at me, confused.

"What are you talking about?" Jean asked. "We haven't seen the punk all day."

"I know what you did to him," I said.

"He's crazy. That's from eating too much rice," Jacques said.

"How could we do anything to him? He wasn't at school today."

"Stop lying," I said. "I'll tell everyone about the rifle if you don't tell me where you put Remi."

Jacques shook his head. "I'm telling you we didn't see the guy."

Jacques looked pale, while Jean seemed ready to throw up.

"Let me out of this cupboard," I ordered. I wanted to see how much power I had over the brothers.

Jean and Jacques pushed each other out of the way to help me. They apologized for keeping me inside the cupboard for so long, and they sounded sincere. When I was finally free of the cupboard, I stretched out the cramps that wracked my body.

Again, I demanded, "Tell me where Remi is."

"I swear on crossed hockey sticks," said Jean. "We didn't see him today."

"He didn't come to school. You have to believe us," offered Jacques.

The brothers trembled before me. They were telling the truth. But this sparked a new mystery. Why hadn't they seen Remi? I thought Father Sasseville's altar boys played some part in Remi's brain-napping. And yet, they had no idea where my friend was.

The only person who would know was the Night Watchman.

SIXTEEN

The church doors were unlocked, but I didn't see Father Sasseville anywhere inside. I suspected he might have been hiding in the bowels of the church, where he was probably scooping out Remi's brains. I searched all over the main floor for stairs or trap doors. I checked between and under the hard wooden benches that lined the church. Above me, a giant mural of Jesus watched from the domed ceiling. I could almost feel his eyes following me.

As I took in the mural, I started to get a sense of just how big the church was. I felt puny against the giant mural and the towering stained glass windows. There could be a million places in the church to hide a brainless body.

Suddenly, a door creaked open to the left of me. A skinny woman in a heavy winter coat exited a large booth. She headed to the front pew, knelt, made a strange motion in front of her chest and then bowed her head. She started to mutter. I tiptoed over to hear what she was saying. It was some kind of chant that she repeated over and over again.

I had no idea what she was saying, but it seemed too important to interrupt. Maybe the booth she came from would have answers. I tiptoed over and cracked the door open. I saw nothing but a dim booth.

"Come inside," Father Sasseville's voice whispered from nearby.

I had found the Night Watchman at last. And with a little luck, I'd soon find Remi too. I stepped inside and looked around for the source of Father Sasseville's voice. The area appeared to be a dark phone booth with a tiny bench, except there was no phone. Instead, a dark mesh screen sat on a wall.

"I am here for you," Father Sasseville said through the screen.

I couldn't see Father Sasseville's face at all. It was too dark. I assumed he couldn't see my face either, which gave me an advantage.

"Whenever you're ready, I'll be listening," he urged.

I sat on the bench and collected my thoughts. This was my big moment. Whatever happened in this booth would determine the future of Earth.

Father Sasseville said. "Do you seek absolution?"

I didn't know what he meant at first. I tried to break the word into smaller parts. "Absolut" was like "absolute," which meant total, but total what? Total failure. The Night Watchman taunted me. I had failed Remi and the rest of the humans on the planet.

I looked around the booth for some sign that I could still stop the invasion, but all I saw was the Night Watchman's shadow against the screen. My head drooped in defeat.

Then something caught my eye. At the bottom of the screen, someone had scratched the word: "Duh." It was Remi's favourite saying. He had sent me a message.

I didn't have to stop the invasion right now. All I had to do was find Remi. If I could do that, then together we could figure out what to do next. In the same way that I broke big words into little parts, I had to split the task of saving the world into little parts. Step one: rescue my friend. Step two: ask Remi what to do. I divided the word "absolution" in a brand new way. "AB" was a blood type for humans. "Solution" was an answer. And I had the human answer to the alien invasion.

"I'm ready," I said.

"What do you have to confess?"

"Don't you hate keeping secrets?"

"Whatever you say will not go beyond this confessional, my son."

"You must know a lot of secrets about a lot of people."

"We're here to talk about your sins."

"Are we?" I asked. "I think you have a few secrets of your own."

Father Sasseville went silent.

I pushed on. "I know what you are doing."

"And what would that be?" He sounded shaky.

"You're planning an invasion."

"Excuse me?"

"I know everything. You're bringing aliens to this town."

"How did you know about that?" Father Sasseville was against the ropes.

"I know about the alien invasion."

"Please, my son. It's rude to call them aliens." He sounded desperate now that his cover was blown. "They're called Vietnamese. They are refugees that need our love and understanding, not our hate."

"Yeah, so they can take over the world."

"They are coming here to start over. You should not have any prejudice against them. They only want to have what we have."

"They want Earth bodies," I accused.

"Earth what? Just what are you talking about?"

"Father Sasseville, I know your plans with my dad."

"Who is your — ? Wait a minute. Are you George Chan's boy?"

"Yes."

"My son, of all people, you should be the most pleased. They're just like you."

I didn't have anything in common with aliens. I felt more human than Saturnian. "I don't want them here."

"But they have a daughter your age and a son who is only a year younger than you. You will become good friends."

"I had a friend, until you took him away."

"I'm afraid I don't know who you're talking about."

"Remi Boudreau."

"Ah, yes. Remi. He's got a good head on his shoulders."

"Not any more."

"What?"

"He's my friend, and I want him back."

"I don't know where he is."

"I know what you're doing. I know why those aliens are coming here. You can call off the invasion."

"My son, why are you so scared? These people have done you no harm."

"They will."

"They won't. They are like you in many ways. They are from the same part of the world as you. Maybe not the same country, but you will have many similarities." He tried to make the invasion sound like it was supposed to be a good thing.

"It's still an invasion," I argued.

"Four people do not make an invasion, my son."

"There will be more. There always is."

"And we will welcome them all with open arms," Father Sasseville said. "If we close our arms, we close our minds."

"I won't let you go through with your plans."

"Don't you want to be with people like you?"

Father Sasseville stumped me. Before I had met Remi I wished that I looked like the other kids at school or that they looked like me. If we looked alike, then I wouldn't feel so alone. But Remi didn't care what I looked like and I didn't care what he looked like, and we were still friends.

"You can't be sure we'll like each other even if we look alike," I argued.

"You haven't even given them a chance."

"I don't want them here. They're going to change everything."

"Sometimes change is a good thing." This guy had an answer for everything.

"I'll tell my parents everything. They'll stop the invasion. They'll see how upset I am and they'll change their minds. I'll make them stop the invasion."

"Perhaps we should talk with them together. I'm sure we can work things out."

Father Sasseville sounded so confident, like he knew my parents would side with him. I started to think about how Mom had pushed Remi out of the store and how Dad never seemed to have time for me.

"I'll go to the newspapers," I said. "I know a magazine that would be very interested in what you're doing."

"We're trying to keep this quiet. We want people to get used to the newcomers on their own terms."

"No one's going to get used to them. They're horrible aliens."

"My son, these people have been through so much already. We should let them come in peace."

"Why? So they can take over people?"

"Take over people? Ah, do you mean they'll take your place?"

I never thought that my parents would replace me because I was an alien like them. Now I knew I was expendable.

"At least return the brains and the aliens can come here."

"Pardon me?"

"You heard me."

"What brains?"

"Remi's brain. And Trina's too. You can keep Eric's."

"I'm afraid I don't understand."

"That's my offer. You have until tomorrow to decide. If not, then I tell everyone about the invasion." I got up and bolted out of the booth. Father Sasseville stepped out of his cubicle and called after me, but I sprinted out of the church.

When I got to the store, Dad and Mom were waiting for me. They didn't look too happy. Father Sasseville must have used some kind of super-advanced alien communication device to tell my parents everything.

"I just got off the phone with the Father," Dad said. "You okay, Marty?"

"Everything will be okay if he does what I say."

Mom felt my forehead. "He not have a fever."

"I'll be fine when Remi comes back."

Mom looked at Dad and shook her head. "That boy no good."

"He's my friend, Mom."

"You not need that kind of friend," she said.

Before she could say anything else Dad stopped her. "Maybe he does."

Mom glared at him. "We talk about this later. Marty, go to your room!"

She used her mind control glare on Dad. He tried to say something, but the words died in his throat. He sat down and looked away from me. Mom motioned me to go to my room.

"But . . . " I said.

"No more talk," Mom barked. She glared at me and turned up the juice on her mind control powers.

I felt compelled to go to my room. I felt powerless against my angry alien mother. It was over. Soon, the aliens would invade and Remi's brain would be lost in a freezer full of human brains.

What made me feel horrible was the fact that I couldn't save Remi. I had known him for less than a week, but I missed him more than I missed Trina. I missed him more than I missed my Saturn home. I missed him more than anything in my entire life. Before I met Remi, I could make it through months without needing to talk to anyone. I got used to being by myself. But now I felt a big, gaping, empty hole inside my chest. And the worst thing was that it had always been there. I just didn't notice it until now.

I tried to read my Hardy Boys book to take my mind off everything, but something had changed. Before, books could transport me to another world where people had lots of friends and set off on great adventures. But now the friends in the book seemed so fake. Some writer had just come up with his idea of what friends should be like. I knew what real friends were. They were the people who filled the hole inside my chest. And my friend was gone.

Seventeen

The next day, I expected to see aliens crawling all over the school. Instead, I saw the French/English alliance prowl the schoolyard. I worried that they might pick on me, but Jacques and Jean had told everyone I was off limits. At least, I had scored one small victory. The kids played together, probably for the last time — as humans.

Eric Johnson and Trina Brewster returned to school. I assumed the aliens had taken them. I talked to Eric in alienese.

"So you're here to take over," I said. *"Does your brain rattle around in that big empty head?"*

Eric screwed up his puzzled face and spat out in English, "Loser."

He walked away. If he had the brain of an alien, why didn't he understand me?

Trina snuck up behind me and shyly said, "Did you notice I wasn't in class?"

I nodded.

She smiled. "It's because I had the flu, but I'm okay now." She wiped her runny nose and sniffled.

"I'm sure you're feeling out of this world," I said.

She didn't understand my dig. Instead, she asked, "I was wondering if I could borrow your notes. Or maybe you could help me catch up on my homework. That is if you want to."

I missed the old Trina, the one who teased me and made my life miserable. I hated this alien Trina who pretended to like me.

I said, "You'll never get my notes. Never. You're a terrible thing."

She huffed, "I thought you were a hero when you saved me from those French kids, but you're just a jerk."

She started to tear up. I was stunned. Suddenly, it dawned on me. How could this alien Trina know that I had saved the real Trina? There could be no way, which meant I had just insulted the real Trina.

"You freak-a-zoid," she said. I had never heard such a sweet sounding word.

Before I could apologize to the real Trina, she stormed off. I ran after her, but I stopped when the other girls giggled at us. I walked away from Trina and sauntered through the schoolyard where the human students played.

The aliens had not taken over my classmates. Trina and Eric had returned to school safe and sound. I wondered if I had single-handedly beaten back the alien invasion. I wondered who else I had saved.

At recess, I looked for Remi all over the schoolyard. I stopped to watch a new war start up. The French kids teamed up with the Anglais to launch an attack on the older students. The opponents weren't divided by language now. They were divided by grade. And the war wasn't so mean-spirited now; it seemed more like a game. Everyone was laughing.

Remi was not among them.

I left the laughing students. I leaned against the Jesus statue and waited for recess to end, alone.

Later that day, at the store, Father Sasseville talked to my mom and dad. Beside him stood a man, a woman, and two kids. These people had black hair and yellow skin. They looked like me except they were all really skinny. It was the first time I had ever seen anyone like me in Bouvier. I had seen pictures, but the people with Father Sasseville were real. I thought I should feel less alone now that I was with people like me, but the hole in my chest still felt huge. It was about the size of Remi Boudreau.

Father Sasseville introduced me, "Marty, these are the Vietnamese refugees. They are your new friends."

"Hi," I grunted.

They nodded at me, but said nothing.

"They don't speak English," Father Sasseville said. "But they'll learn."

The aliens had arrived, but not in the brains of my schoolmates. Maybe the alien invasion plan was to move to Bouvier and live here among the humans.

"Shall we go, George?" Father Sasseville asked.

My dad nodded. He led the aliens out of the store.

"Where are they going?" I asked Mom.

"They go to new home in city."

"They're not staying here?

"No. We think it better they live in city. The church find other people to take them in."

"They're not going to take over the town?"

Mom shook her head. I watched the aliens leave in Dad's car. As quickly as it had started, the invasion was over. I had won. But the price I paid was my friend Remi.

I shambled to my room and flopped on my bed. Nothing made sense. I was alone again. I wished I could make my life right again, but I hadn't learned how to do that yet.

Suddenly, there was a thump on my bedroom wall. There were two more thumps. A pause. Then two thumps, four raps, a dog bark, and seventeen rapid thumps. Remi's secret signal. I sprang from the bed and ran to the back door. Remi stood there as if nothing had happened to him.

"Is it you?" I asked.

"Duh? Who else would it be?"

I knocked on his head. "Is it yours?"

"Ow." He knocked my head in retaliation.

It was definitely Remi.

"Your mom called my mom and said it was okay for me to come over."

I couldn't believe that my mom had done this. Why would she let Remi come back? Did she like this human? Was I wrong when I thought that she cared more about other aliens than she cared about me? Why was I wasting my time thinking about her when my best friend had returned?

I smiled at Remi, "The invasion's over."

"It is?"

"I stopped it," I said.

"How?"

"Come in, and I'll tell you all about it."